THE NEW BIZARRO AUTHOR SER
PRESENTS

IR

F4

LARISSA GLASSER

ERASERHEAD PRESS
PORTLAND, OREGON

ERASERHEAD PRESS
P.O. BOX 10065
PORTLAND, OR 97296

www.eraserheadpress.com
facebook/eraserheadpress

ISBN: 978-1-62105-253-1
Copyright © 2018 by Larissa Glasser
Cover design copyright © 2018 Eraserhead Press

Printed in the USA.

EDITOR'S NOTE

Potential is a funny thing. We fear it, we crave it, and we hesitate to bring it out. We cannot live without it and it is likely to protect us as it is to kill us. Larissa Glasser's F4 is a pain-filled story of a woman on a ship on the back of a sleeping monster, a woman whose own potential has slumbered deep inside her for so long, whose self has been suppressed. F4 might be about the trans experience but that doesn't mean it's about slapping you in the face with politics. This is a story full of monsters, magic, dimensional rifts, and madness, sweet madness. You're about to embark on a cruise, destination truly unknown.

–Garrett Cook, editor

for Fiona,
my 25th-hour kaiju muse

PART ONE

/PROLOGUE/

These newest lessons are brought to you by the letter F and the number four. F is a hilarious letter—the sixth letter of our alphabet has a special talent for sailing our minds into the gutter. Sometimes we take the pornographic ambition of language for granted. But crowdsource the hivemind and you'll see for yourself. I did that one time on the interwebz, and I got thousands of suggestions: Fart, fondle, fap, felch—I mean, shit there are some great ways to fuck with language. It depends on what agenda we're trying to cram down the throat of a universe thirsty for hallucinogens, desperate living, and girldick. Language can also be used for shitty purposes that I had to fight against, even though I don't fully understand exactly why at the time. I'm still looking for an answer to some of that.

But let's start with brass tacks first—this very ship, The Finasteride, *Maid of the Seas*, is built from the finest grade dura-steel, surgically grafted into the mottled flesh and bones of the large-scale aggressor-beast known only F4. This was the fourth kaiju to visit us and crush our cities into dust and paste. F4 is the most famous of them all, not only because it leveled New York City with just one flip of its tail, but because it had a personal connection with me, of all people.

I had moved away from Brooklyn by the time it hit, but my dick still likes to get wise with me when it reiterates that F4 was actually just trying to find me, like a lost child in a mall, and finally had thrown a shitfit when it realized I had gone.

Everyone wants to know about the precise mechanics of how this trip works and what the power is behind it. When the coalition finally managed to sedate F4 with the gasbomb of [REDACTED], the freelance team of surgeons, veterinarians, and cryptozoologists set to work with a meticulously rehearsed, cold efficiency. They worked in shifts with massive hyper-cranes and bus-sized scalpels to slice the beast's flesh open at designated areas and graft the preassembled frame of The Finasteride into F4's gray-green body, all along a grid marked into the body with fluorescent ink. This was going to be the proving ground for Regalia Corporate, which never took maybe for an answer.

They had to work very fast for each component, because the flesh of this beast healed much more quickly than that of F3, their previous surgery and a source of profound embarrassment. Determined to not make the same mistakes, the team eschewed safety for the sake of strength and speed—there were indeed a few casualties but of course these were non-union workers. After they lobotomized the creature, they installed the links of

Metasequoia-sized control rods into the beast's rectum, kidneys, shoulders, and fins. Other than the bone-grafting, there was no need for stitching nor staples because the monster's flesh sealed over the components within moments of installation. Surgeons stood in awe as this happened, like watching a time-lapse sequence of ultra-terrestrial conception. We were giving birth to our own version of what we'd wanted the monster to be, now that we seemed to be in control.

Here was living proof of medical innovation and entrepreneurial spirit's ability to conquer nature. Then, came the most challenging stage of grafting the interior of the ship into the monster's nervous system, then alongside the digestive tract, to and through the glistening muscle, and finally, installing the luxury casino multiplex into its unfortunate spleen.

Finally, once all the other components were installed and their pivots stress-tested, the surgery team of Regalia Corporate delivered the coup de grace with the installation of The Leonardo, a 1000-foot broadcast antenna whose range reach even beyond the sun itself and still maintain its basic integrity of signal, also served as nervous system regulator, a delivery device for measured doses of [REDACTED] to assure the beast stayed functionally unconscious, and also—at its zenith—a penthouse for the highest paying customers who wanted a lot of privacy and a great view of the atrocities below.

But in the interest of full corporate transparency, you the passengers are well within your rights when you ask where we are and how we got here. If you behave yourselves and sit quietly, I assure you, we'll get to the bottom of everything. There might be a quiz later.

/01/

The Finasteride was about to finally launch from Raneiri, the most volcanically active island of The Caribbean, and the most also queerphobic, a true vestige of British colonialism. Shore leave had been fun, regardless. Chloe and I had hatched a few eggs who had heard we'd arrived like trans femme self-help showgirls from Vegas. When President Raneiri had gotten wind of us and sent his secret police to round us all up, we'd already brought about seven refugees on board The Finasteride and as soon as the troops saw the reality of F4, the massive final kaiju, its reality eclipsed the legend and the fuckers ran screaming back to the Presidential palace. Even in its dormant state, the monster instilled fear in the people who deserve to be made afraid.

That day of our launch homeward was my first time camming on board the ship. It was Chloe's setup. She had nice equipment, I think she'd either conned someone out of it or she'd spent all her earnings from her lecture tours about her decades in sex work, how she'd made three hardline senators decide to hatch, and the fluid dynamics of post-orchiectomy penetration. She wasn't simply a star for her looks but devoted considerable time to smacking down the ire she drew from TERFs. Chloe was not one to be gaslit, which I loved most of all. She made her enemies want to drink their own piss.

I loved her, body and mind, even if she still intimidated me.

I felt nervous because I didn't really know who was watching our footage on the mainland. I hoped some were potential employers. I knew my parents wouldn't be seeing it.

This toothless guy named Janssen was on his knees before me, wearing full Carol Channing makeup complete with hoop earrings, and dressed like a mummy enshrouded in cling wrap. He was furiously gumming my nutsack, which had deflated from my year-old orchie. The skin was stretching with this activity. With no teeth in his mouth to block it, his saliva pooled into my ass crack and began flood onto my anus, forming a thin membrane of humiliation for him and dysphoria for me. The camera wouldn't catch that, but it felt foreign and awkward, regardless. I convinced myself if I impressed Chloe she'd fuck my throat so hard it would garble my attempts to praise her. I was hungry for something more, for her, because I'd become convinced by then that cis people are bad luck. I knew from experience.

Chloe kept hissing at me to get harder and to squeal more, repeating bullet-point missives from her own decade-old voice feminization instruction DVDs. I glanced up at the camera, its solid red 'ON' light eating me raw, better than Janssen. I wasn't into cis guys anymore, but I wanted to do a good job for Chloe. I finally managed to force a grin as I remembered that I'd once been a suit-and-tie minion at a Manhattan auditing firm.

I had definitely leveled-up from that.

My tongue flecked my upper front teeth to clean up any stray, overdone lipstick. At the far, wood-paneled wall of my cabin, Chloe sat in her old-school director's chair. She wore those huge Lemmy mirror-aviator shades, so it was hard to tell if she was looking at me, Janssen, or if she was just staring into the ether. She been on adanaC-grade hallucinogens since the start of the cruise, but I guess she was functional enough to direct us. She was dressed in this really cool black leather power suit with silver piping just like the kind she once wore onstage. She knew all the new hatches in the audience thought she looked red-hot, a miracle of what plastic surgery and a little confidence could accomplish in a hostile-cis world. She'd been a cottage industry out of both her academic study and her 'how to pass' curricula. Everyone was so desperate to blend in back then. She looked as smoking trans femme-hot as ever. I finally got hard with the thought of finally being allowed to suck *her* prick, even though I still had most of my teeth. Actually, I wanted to tap Janssen aside, unfasten Chloe from the bottom up, undo her tuck and spit-rub our clits together until we flooded her suite with a torrent of girl-cum. That would be a true cam moment, something the audience actually wanted and deserved. I'd wanted her for years, but had always felt wrong for objectifying her from way back in the audience when I hadn't even hatched yet.

Chloe lowered her sunglasses, smiled back at me, and gave me a thumbs-up as she snorted some more adanaC from a small Altoids tin. My junk was ready for primetime, apparently, as it bulged and throbbed with each up-suck and dive from the toothless mummy-sub. As he was smoking my pole, I was thinking of how high Chloe was getting. By that time, though, Janssen's drool was flooding onto my asshole in a torrent, and the sheets were getting soaked.

I flipped Chloe off.

"Don't give *that* much to edit out, Carol," she scolded me. "Things get too choppy, and that's more work for me." I opened my mouth to speak but Chloe gestured for me to shut up.

"Will you just not talk," she directed, "and start making the whore-moans like we said?"

I reached deep inside, tried to keep thinking of being topped by my mentor instead of Janssen tonguing my sack. I wanted to do right by Chloe, and her viewers, so I started breathing more quickly, emitting highly pitched gasps and squeals I tried to remember from her voice instruction DVDs. I tried to imagine Chloe sticking her prick in my ass so hard that the tip of her clit would reach all the way forward to my soft palate and I could inverse-blow her while she was inside my body. I had a searing case of hot for teacher. So much had come full circle, all of the conflicted signals of wanting to fuck or be women, but then only wanting to be with true women who had been through similar trajectories. It was a pretty meta desire, one that leftist theorists and sexologists still have a ball with. None of us care, as long as we get to find someone we like and get to make out and fuck. Sometimes it works out well. It hasn't for me yet, although it's a star I still chase like an idiot.

So anyway, Janssen was the only toothless guy we knew of on the ship. His mouth was like this little tentacle—little suction divots where his teeth used to be—as he worked my tissue. Chloe wanted to set him up as a mermaid, so he could work my thighs, but we'd decided to keep things simple for the first throw.

She'd told me I'd be getting a handsome cut if these videos hit as well as they were supposed to. She'd had pre-orders, because of Chloe's and my combined star power. There were even some pro-wrestling fans who tuned in just for rare access to see me naked.

"Tongue her shaft, Janssen," she directed. "We need more from you, fuckhead! Do I have to hold a gun to your head? Remember, you wanted the scholarship! Now you have to do the *work*!"

Chloe actually did have a really good SIG-sauer she kept with the rest of her gear. I figured it would come in handy at some point, especially if anyone had found out we were going to rob the casino.

Janssen looked up at me, contrition in his wide blue eyes, wormed up a few inches, and rotated his head so he could manage a better suck-angle. His tongue just felt clammy, not well-studded, unremarkable as it slowly lathered the underside of my dick, then retracted for a new ascent along the same track. I was *so* not into chasers, but I tried to keep thinking of being anally skewered by Chloe's pikestaff, Cannibal Holocaust-style. That's what kept me hardish, to be honest.

I'd never asked Janssen how he lost his teeth, he was

kind of young, but who knows with this world. Maybe he wanted them removed at the dentist just to perform this activity on me. Chloe tells me that gumming's a new thing in trans porn, so I took her word for it. The fact that Janssen volunteered so readily made me think I had bigger notoriety than I'd thought.

The Finasteride began to clang at slow but steady intervals, and the floor and bed resonated as the pistons of ship's engines began to initiate their syncopated balladry. We'd be put back to sea soon for our return journey to the mainland, so I figured we'd better hurry up while the cabin floor was still level enough to cam.

Just then, there was a loud set of knocks at the door, someone using the base of their palm to broadcast some sort of urgency.

A voice came through the door, "*Carol!*"

Chrissakes, it was Roz. My sister was the reason I even had that crummy job (the official one). This Chloe thing was a side gig but I'd wanted to think it was so much more than that.

But Roz was getting up in our shit again.

"*FUCK!*" Chloe spewed as she got up from her director's chair, and shoved it back. She pressed a button behind the camera and the red record-light flashed in standby mode. Janssen broke free from my crotch and squirmed aside, tried to hide behind the bed, and began to falsetto Meat Loaf's "Paradise by the Dashboard Light" in a breathy approximation of Candy Darling. I suspect my path had been somewhat similar to Janssen's, but we were different enough for me to not give a shit about his level of discomfort. Just trans or GTFO because fuck "ready."

"Just see what she wants," Chloe whispered to me.

"We're taking off, anyway," I told her. "We'll try camming again later."

"This took a lot of setup, Carol."

I shrugged, got up, and threw on a simple cotton robe. The logo of The Finasteride was embroidered on its left tit.

"We have to get the bar girls ready, anyway."

"Please," Janssen finally said, his speech slurred by his bare gums. "Hide me."

"You don't tell us what to do," Chloe told him. "Your casino debt gives us at least 600 hours of your gumjobs, plus whatever other Little Bo Peep shit we decide for you."

The little dude was getting stiff again with Chloe's invectives. It was like he was having the best wet dream. Janssen certainly wasn't boring trade.

"Once you've paid it off," she went on, "that's when you can ask permission to piss."

"Look, I'll just go see what my sister wants, okay?" I told them, and then told Janssen to just stop mewling.

I opened the cabin door just a crack and squeezed into the hallway. Roz was standing there, trying to peer in. She was already wearing her crew uniform, even though we hadn't raised anchor yet. Her auburn hair was tied up and if I hadn't known any better, I'd have thought she really was trying to cosplay Jill Whelan from "The Love Boat," mousy and proper. My sister had always been a little shorter than me. I stood up on my toes to get even taller, then nudged her to face the other way.

"Come on," I rolled my eyes at her. "What do you

need, I'm super-busy right now."

"Come on, yourself."

She turned everything I said back at me—she'd done that since we were little, even before I'd started *borrowing* her clothes.

"Can't you see we need to get back to work? The passengers are going to mob the casino."

I told her most of them were just going to get settled in their cabins to freshen up, put their masks on, and puke enough into their private shit-pipes to leave room for the night's buffet, drinks from my girldick waitstaff, adanaC dosages from my girldick waitstaff, girldick dosages from my adanaC waitstaff, all spent in a haze of pseudo-understanding/allyship that would strike just enough balance for them in their denial haze to feel like normal and real passengers rather than debauched, rich, non-hatching 1%-ers.

I told Roz we had plenty of time to set up. But she was right in that I needed the head start, because I had an entire staff of trans barmaids to muster. Many of them were going to be hungover from shore leave and on hardcore adanaC. All good, I was going to be on some, too. The trip back was always a ramp-up in activity, because the degenerate gamblers wanted to party like fuck before the journey on The Finasteride ended.

"So," Roz asked me. "Are you going to brief with Captain Brock looking like that?"

"What are you even? The sooner you let me get dressed, the sooner I can go get that over with."

"I heard that the revenue from the casino was down," she said quietly, not looking at me directly. "Corporate's not going to like that too much."

"What, did they FAX you something?"

"No, Carol. I've been on these cruises before. This is your first time out, remember?"

I couldn't argue that point with her.

"Just try not to get in a lot of trouble with Brock," she said. "I know he's old-school and entitled, but remember why you're here, okay?"

This was Roz's first trip out with Brock, so I didn't know why that gave her more of a line on him than me, by then. But I didn't want to argue with her. Janssen's drool had dried on my perineum and upper thighs, and it felt gross. I just wanted to wash it off. The thought of Chloe then counteracted and got me hard again. I shifted into myself.

"Corporate's probably going to ask you to re-mix the drinks or reconfigure your staff," she said. "Just be ready for anything. Quintal's also going to try and micro-manage you."

"I ignore everything that fuck says."

My sisters rolled her eyes and backed away.

"Look, this is the gig we were assigned," Roz went on. "Just try to get us all back to the mainland without any more of your overcompensated 'trans power' bullshit? Okay?"

I didn't say anything.

"That a *possibility*?" she called to me after she'd turned the corner and then said some other things I didn't catch as she faded into the distance. I think I just wasn't listening to her closely enough by then.

They say that once you've taken a trip on the Finasteride, you're a changed person. Nothing will ever be the same.

Everything you ever longed for becomes a reality, and everything you ever feared and hated then becomes your fantasy. But once you're back in the world, at your home, and your job, nothing works out in the end. Too late, we have your money (well, Regalia has it). And you'll keep coming back for another ride on the back and in the belly, intestines, bowels, and rectum of the beast.

So many of them had bought into the latest ad campaign puked forth by Regalia Corporation—that The Finasteride was "luxury redefined."

So along with the martini baths, girldick seaweed wraps, cockfights, human cockfights, pre-assigned gambling allotment no-limit lottery, and grindhouse dips into the very lymph-baths of F4 itself (The Fountain of Youth), you could say that people come to The Finasteride for an experience like no other.

Because we offer an experience no one else on Earth can offer.

And everyone is asking to be The Middle Piece of the kaiju centipede.

We are stapled and sewn onto and within Fury-beast four.

So fasten your seatbelts, ladies.

You are in for the fuck-ride of your lives.

F4.

/02/

*S*hit, I thought as the ship convulsed during my journey down to the Captain Gerhard Brock's suite. *We almost woke it up that time. We shouldn't even say its name.*

The party in there had started without me. The table was strewn with a massive buffet of starch and pastries. The flies had already come to settle on the amenities, but these weren't ordinary North American houseflies—these were *Raneiri* flies, a special hybrid grown from the labs of its centuries–old colonizers. They average the size of a child's fist, but these one were definitely big fuckers as they alighted upon the buffet of steak slices from F4 itself, iced buckets of crab-dog legs sticking out like Sarlaac vajayjays, and a melting chocolate ice cream cake that ran along the tabletop in the humid air. It felt like the walls were melting, along with the cake. I didn't bother to ask why the AC wasn't running. No one got up when I entered the room. Not seen as a lady.

Stately and smug, Captain Brock looked like he'd

swallowed about five pounds of whipped nougat, but it hadn't travelled all the way into his stomach. His forehead also looked bigger than I'd last seen him, pregnant beneath the crude white lighting. He seemed to have outgrown his clothes, and I could feel a colder than usual scrutiny from him as he sat at the head of a long Wal-Mart table that offset the semi-posh surroundings of the suite. I gently kicked a leg of a table leg, and the wobble sent Raneiri-flies buzzing about in an aimless quasi-panic. I swatted a few away from my head with a paper napkin.

Behind Brock, there hung the head of a purple stuffed baseball mascot, as if one of those big muppets that met an untimely end by breathing Brock's B.O. His pits were sweating copiously and corroding the threads of his admiralty jacket, celebrating their toxicity in the Caribbean soup. The whole place reeked of the rotting beef you notice coming from an Arby's dumpster.

That's also what seeing Eduoard Quintal reminded me of. Much smaller than Brock and more stringy, as if his head and feet had been taffy-pulled by a giant child, He was sitting at Brock's right and smirked at me. Quintal was Ship's Master but I didn't take any orders from him unless Brock demanded it so. Maybe that was why I was being called in.

I'd done my best to dress conservatively, trying to model myself after Chloe despite her underlying kinkiness and lasciviousness, her appeal to the universal repressed cis desire to fuck us. My tuck was sweating like hell and it was a wreck. Just what I needed.

I was relieved a little when they finally invited me to sit.

I came down into the chair at a careful angle.

"We're expected to arrive in Miami in just over two days," Brock told us. His voice sounded hoarse, like he'd spent the last interval arguing with a hundred people at once. "I got off the phone with our liaison at Regalia head office. We're going to need you to keep the bar open longer, Carol. The casino revenue has plateaued. We need you to step up the action."

Quintal joined in, his voice an unpleasant tremulant whine. "Actually we need to make twice as much during the return trip."

I leaned in. I'd worked doubles plenty of times before, but never with so little staff. Some of the trans girls on my shifts actually needed time to dilate and all that fun stuff. That could take up an entire shift sometimes, from what I'd been told, especially on rough seas.

"From what I hear," Quintal sneered, "they don't need to dilate if they take enough big dick. That takes care of everything, including the increased revenue. Two birds, one stone!"

He thought I was going to whore out my girls just because he suggested it. I had stipulated to them long before, we'd only do such things if we wanted to, and on our own terms.

"You ever fuck one of us," I asked him, "and been able to keep it up for more than two seconds? How do these chain smoking, coked-out gamblers maintain a hard on when they can't even beat off? Maybe if they were fucking *your* pussy, on the other hand…"

Normally I wasn't that crude but the fact that Brock hadn't reined him in pissed me off. But I knew the pecking order well enough.

Brock just snickered like he was watching something

from the Springer archives and shook his head.

"Let's just focus on the logistics of the return trip," he commanded.

"Why isn't Chloe here?" I asked, then. "She runs the casino, I just keep the staff."

"We're replacing her with you."

By the time I was done trying to floss the pubes from between my teeth, I figured any open air was better than breathing the processed fetor of the ship. Even with the filters in place, we were all still breathing the bodily functions of a biological entity, the dura-steel framework of The Finasteride, no matter how miraculous its technical atrocity, was only a tool compared to the membranes that surrounded it. Remember that old Conan the Barbarian chestnut, The Riddle of Steel?—*flesh is stronger*. I'd once heard a noise band write a whole song about how Conan had just been an egg. That had made plenty of sense to me.

I felt desperate to clear my head and to not think about the petty politics on board. They didn't mean much in the grand scheme of things. But I had to abide the situation regardless, accept the self-contained world of the vessel, the sudden lurches of The Finasteride as she gave measured electric shocks to the anus, shoulders, and fins of the creature, so it would swim with a sort of muscle memory like a gargantuan toad, smooth and mellow but also sometimes jerky and spastic. Sometimes you could predict the rhythms of the lurches and spasms as we sprayed from the Caribbean in powerdrive mode, riding the back of a sleeping giant. But you never got quite used to it. Dilating on board must have been fun for the post-op girls on my team. That was why so many had not opted for shore leave on Raneiri—they'd taken the opportunity to regimen themselves on calm waters.

The afternoon waned as I climbed up onto the topmost deck and made my way by slow, steady increments up toward the front of the ship. Even though the scrub crew had made their formidable rounds throughout the night and morning, I still had to shuffle through plenty of detritus of the debauch, typically crushed plastic cups, crumpled bikini tops and bottoms (often with the crotches scissored out for easier access to our pricks, because sometimes they want us to keep as many articles of our clothing on during sex for the sake of maintaining their own crossdress fantasies), spewey'd condoms, little unfolded wax paper wrappers people used to dose adanaC, emptied mini-bottles of sunscreen passengers had used for lube-often with dried-brown shit-streaks on the white plastic housing. Most of this trash baked in the sun, unattended, giving off a fetor of something Vegas could never aspire to.

I kicked a forgotten dildo into a huge cluster of shit that been left in the middle of the deck, turned a corner, and found Chloe there at the prow. She was thumbing at her phone and ignoring the grand horizon. It was easier to breathe out in the ocean winds, but there was still an oppressiveness about us as the crab-dog parasites secreted from F4's outer dermis swung about from the upper bulkheads. Their trajectories were easy enough to anticipate and dodge but you needed to be hyper-aware of your surroundings up there. Some of the creatures would deliberately aim for your head as they descended, others would glide over and aim poop drops into your cleavage. Sometimes both.

Chloe didn't wait for me to speak.

"It's totally fine with me, Carol."

She looked me in the eye, finally. I told her I don't know why they'd shifted our stations around in the middle of the trip.

"To separate us," she said. "They know I hacked my way into the satellite dishes, for the camming unlink. They tried to put in a new encryption in The Leonardo, but I chewed my way through that shit in like two minutes."

"I guess that's the end of our supplemental income for this trip."

"Look, it doesn't bother me, we both have better things ahead. In less than three days we're set to go, we'll be working together on our own terms. We'll be our own bosses, finally."

She turned to the water. I stood close behind her, my prick hard against her asscrack, realizing we looked like we were pseudo-cosplaying Leonardo and Kate from "Titanic."

"And besides," she went on. "Did they give you any paperwork to sign? Anything by Regalia that changes your job status or mine?"

Brock hadn't shown me anything like that at all.

"So? There's no change in payscale, no change in hours. It's just a petty power play from the boys. Nothing's really changed."

"Incoming, *heads up*."

A crab-dog zipped down and one of its tendrils caught on Chloe's hair. It hung there, writhing and squeaking, the weight of it bringing Chloe's head down almost to the railing.

"*Motherfuck!*" she hissed. "Son of a—Carol, *come on*! HELP ME!"

Her cry was cut short as the parasite dug its claws deeper into the side of her head, unleashed a spiky proboscis from its belly, jammed it into her mouth, and began fucking the hole with the giddy aplomb of an misty-eyed egg discovering trans porn for the first time.

I didn't want to touch the beast. These things were apparently less lethal with F4 kept in its dormant state, but I'd never tempted fate, nor did I want to. Not even for Chloe. She shook her head violently, but it didn't dislodge its peepee from her mouth. She tried grabbing at it but the thorns made that difficult for her. Maybe it wanted her autograph, but I think it was really not sure what else do with her her, like it wanted to do more but couldn't reconcile its own physicality with her host body.

I moved closer. Before I could get the scissors from my purse, Chloe swatted at the pest and successfully set it free. It wailed during its downfall and splashed into the roiling foam.

"I've never seen one fly this far out on the deck," I told her.

"Who—the fuck, Carol that thing almost threw me overboard!"

Above us, there was a line of crab-dogs peering over the edge. Some of them looked ready to follow their friend's example. Most of them were just licking each other's buttholes, as was their nature. It was a little troubling to see them in such an organized formation, though.

Chloe started to calm down a little, but still seemed like the place is getting to her, like she couldn't get to the mainland soon enough. But I wasn't feeling so excited to go back—it meant the online harassment campaign against me would pick up right where it had left off. Then, abruptly jarring me from my melancholy reprieve, Chloe asked me if I'd discussed my plans with my sister.

"No, I haven't even mentioned it."

Chloe gestured past my shoulder. Roz was standing against the bulkhead a few yards away, glaring at Chloe with her arms crossed.

"Well, now's your chance."

Chloe took off without another word and headed below. She brushed past Roz and both scoffed at each other. I didn't want this to escalate.

Too late, I could tell. This was going to be a long-ass day.

Before I can say anything, Roz told me the gumming footage had been leaked license- and encryption free by The Ratite Cult.

"Fuck," I muttered. "They're still onto me."

"Well, yeah, I told you this would happen," she said. "You're letting Chloe make a fool of you."

"I don't really care what they do with the shot, Roz. I'm glad they saw me. I wanted them to know I got away."

"They've issued a new fatwa against you."

"They can't get to me," I told her as I turned away to watch the far horizon. "I'm not within their reach anymore. Are they going to swim out to us?"

"I don't know what you expect to happen when we get to land. I'm heading right to Regalia HQ to see if they have anything available on a *normal* cruise line."

"I don't know if those are still even docked in Miami," I told her. That much seemed true, and the waiting list to board the next Finasteride trip was already full about five times over limit. Besides, F4 was going to take up almost the entire harbor, and everyone would inevitably be hypnotized by it as it sat anchored. The beast was the main sales pitch for Regalia Corporation—its invincibility and power rubbed off on its passengers, indeed they could live forever after a cruise on the monster's back.

"I can't keep carrying you, Carol," Roz said, looking me in the eye for the first time what seemed like a week. "You're going to have to start making it on your own."

I lowered my voice—it always sounded weird to me, like I wasn't even trying to pass as cis anymore. There was a spark of sad recognition in Roz's face, like she missed her older, miserable brother. As if I was some invading spirit that was squatting in the person she once knew. To be perfectly honest, that's what it felt like sometimes.

"I'm actually thinking of going west with Chloe," I told her. "She's got a good setup in L.A."

Roz shrugged. I'd thought she was going to try and implore me to come to my senses and not go. But she didn't seem surprised at all, as if she'd known what I was going to do before I did.

"Yeah, well. You might just find yourself alone when you get there. Chloe is just going to use you up and then move on to someone younger."

"I don't know what's going to happen." I looked out again at the dwindling sunlight and thought of our parents, stranded somewhere out there in the deep ocean on the other end of the world.

"You think *I* do?"

"I just want to get this trip over with. Brock's got

this weird god complex settling into his head and the casino's going to be fucked up tonight. Everyone's going to be blowing their kids' tuition at the tables, trying to make a go at the final house jackpot. Plus, Quintal's guards are going to be watching us like fuckin' vultures."

"We're all going to be stressed during this return journey," Roz said. "You're not alone in that. Supplies are running low and I have to try to deal with the repercussions of that."

"Let's just try to get through tonight," I told her. "There'll be plenty of answers once we get on shore and find there's nowhere to go but putting back to sea."

"You're going to get sick of it eventually."

I already was.

/03/

W'ed only just opened, and the casino was already at full capacity. Everyone was going to want to blow everything they'd won from their binges during the outbound trip. Now that they were returning home to their jobs, kids, and lost horizons, they were going to go for fucking broke and part at full fuck-tilt. There was a sad urgency to the night, as if it was a final fuck before the guillotine, a frantic and desperate sprint to reach that *divinum raptus* before blowing their kids' college savings, and the last-ditch attempt to save their mortgages.

Even though a lot of my staff had only transitioned in the last year or so, most of them knew how to look after themselves. Regalia didn't know as much about screening help as much as they let on, but I definitely knew where to find talent. I was very maternal towards my bar staff.

As soon as we turned the lights on, all the gears of the passengers' addiction raged like lab rats wanting placebo, rushing and vying for a place at the tables, begging to be liberated from their savings. The clientele would rather starve than not have their pleasure centers 100% lit, every living moment. See, gambling never interested me in the slightest—but after just a week of working the bar team here I understood it a little better than when I was on the mainland. On this, our beast-ship, our most primal natures for instant gratification had free reign, perhaps encouraged by the nature of F4 itself—hungry, angry, lost. The desire for release is always unfulfilled, and we keep trying to find it anyway, always just out of reach. So, we try to keep them distracted from the philosophy of loss with colors and shapes, patterns and pulse of the dancing casino lights, like trout will go after something shiny. My job was to keep the bar girls making steady rounds, to distract the passengers with booze and the occasional surreptitious and incomplete tablecloth handjob, distracted by the next customer to flash a twenty—my barmaids keep them frustrated, aroused and continually spending. It was all about the bottom line, and nothing else.

The music got louder and the place grew even more stuffy and cramped with Quintal's goons patrolling the crowd and stationed at all corners of the complex. These grim-faced lunkheads were way too obvious in the gaudy atmosphere, dressed in trim navy-blue collared shirts and slacks, fabric belts that made them look like former Blockbuster Video employees but with extended magazine-Uzis. They also had like, these Devo haircuts that looked like little plastic wigs. There were still people trying to get in. Chloe stood at the hostess station, wearing this scintillating black leather sheath dress with a scooped back that accentuated the broadness of her shoulders. She stood there impassively filing her nails, paying little heed to the sunscreen-glistened cattle run of people who climbed over or wormed under the velvet rope to get a prime spot at the tables. Some people were asking her where the buffet was but she just pointed them toward the gendered bathrooms.

I knew Chloe wasn't upset at her demotion, because indeed our pay scales hadn't changed, it was more that she didn't need to care as much about running the casino, so I think that was a mixed blessing for her. Brock and Quintal though having the guards there would dissuade any cheating, but I knew their wits were nowhere no as finely tuned as Chloe's. Maybe that was why she had also hinted at robbing the place. I also wonder if that was why they had also taken her off the job. It wouldn't end up mattering much—all I cared about once we got to the mainland was going west with Chloe, finding my people, and destroying the hardwired sexual inhibitions that had kept me from living up to then.

I went behind the bar where I could at least anchor myself to a familiar routine, and wouldn't have to overthink the work. Quintal's forces made me nervous enough, but when the most talented of my barmaids, Barbara, Michette, and Ivanka set the speed, hotness, and attitude example for the rest of my waitstaff, alternating drink orders with feel cops that passed along and were tipped thrice over as required, I wasn't so worried about interference by the toy soldiers. Chloe had helped train my girls so well, many of them weren't even aware they'd be such naturals at it. There's no room for modesty on The Finasteride, and since most of the trans women on board knew the score right at the outset, it only made sense that the casino rounds had to be sink or swim, and we were doing our level best. Hey, Regalia wanted increased revenue, right? We were going to deliver, sure, but on our own fucking terms.

Confident that enough of my girls would manage on their own, I focused on the bar regulars. Pushing down my feeling that something felt *off* tonight by applying myself to mindless drudgery.

The cop was first up, unfortunately. But I figured it was okay to get him out of the way first. He was easy anyway, all he wanted was PBR and an order of pretzel rolls. He kept throwing me a ton of shade, either because he couldn't square his self-perception with the ticket he had purchased, he recognized me from the news, or both. Most likely both. But there wasn't time to parse his damage, it was going to too busy for me to be overly-involved in what some cop thought of me. I took his order, slid his beer over to him, and moved on over to the Old Navy shirt lady. Her drink preferences were even less elaborate than the cop, she usually wanted a Shirley Temple without a cherry—extreme blasphemy, but some cis women really are beyond hope. For food, she usually asked for pork nachos, but on this night she wasn't having any food. I put that down to our fresh run back to the mainland, but I also hoped that didn't mean we had norovirus on the ship—there was something we definitely didn't need.

I was surprised Janssen hadn't shown up yet. He was usually all about his Margaritas, even though he usually couldn't enjoy them fully because he had no teeth, the straw was his friend. But I figured he was probably still trying to process his unfinished business with me and the camming. He'd shown enough bravery for one day, I'd figured.

I then took a few more orders, nothing out of routine, and even though I maintained a comfortable high on adanaC, I was already getting bored. But then my favorite customer Laura broke through the moiling crowd.

Laura and I had some of the more interesting conversations across the counter because she'd worked as a cryptozoologist, and knew more about F4 than anyone at Regalia. I never had time to listen to the full scale of what she told me, but my trans-dar was very well tuned and I found myself drawn more into my girlcrush moreso than any professional interest. Of course, I was still obsessed with Chloe, on a sublimely unhealthy level, but Laura had this simple way of dressing with earthy colors that accentuated her shoulder-length blonde hair. It made her look so prairie-trans, so uncorrupted, my prick couldn't help divining toward that. When you've been through the sort of things I have and have given up everything in the process of surviving, occasionally you manage to admit to yourself when a fantasy hookup feels nice, even if it will never happen. Laura's younger brother Jaden then showed up her side, and that killed my buzz. Since he couldn't have been aged more than twelve or so, the kid didn't really belong there in the complex. But who cared, really? Quintal's forces didn't even notice he was there.

Jaden was this precocious little snot who dominated most of the conversations at the bar. He said he knew more about the intricate hidden passageways of The

Finasteride than about the Beast F4, but despite his precociousness that also was fascinating to listen to. I tried to seem engaged so his sister would stay at the bar longer.

"He's been through all of the ducts," Laura told me. "Little spider monkey."

On this night, though, our first on the journey back to Miami, he had more to offer.

"I found something out tonight," he told us. "Try and guess what."

Laura and I looked at each other and shrugged.

"No," he insisted. "Just guess."

I looked down and decided to fuck with his block.

"You…got pregnant?"

Laura laughed at the ceiling.

"No!" he beamed. "Did you know your ice station leads right into the monster's pancreas?"

The ship shook a little at the live mention of the thing beneath us.

He pointed to the unit behind me. It wasn't a huge fridge, it stood just about tit-height, and I used it a lot for making sure I had my bins full. Jaden encouraged me to try the secret latch. I followed his instructions and found the latch. Sure enough, the ice bin swiveled out to reveal a small tunnel that led into the glowing red of a secret passageway, something right out of Scooby Doo. I told him that was neat, but that it wouldn't help keep the bar running. My remark went over his head, but Laura smiled at me close-lipped. I liked that she was so understated in comparison with our surroundings.

I asked her what she was going to do once she got to Miami. She didn't really know. She was thinking of moving on to Brisbane to study the cultural after-effects of the kaiju-wars there. She'd told me the story, but to actually be on the pummeled ground where it had happened made all the difference to her as a researcher. She said Jaden hadn't been to Australia before.

"I heard it stinks," the kid said.

"Maybe we'll take a boat, rather than fly," she told him. That seemed to please him and shut him up for the time being.

"Just be careful," I told them. "I heard there are crevasses there that have a will of their own."

No sooner had I said this when the list to starboard increased about fifteen degrees within just a few seconds. Chips, drinks, and chairs went flying, as did a lot of my waitstaff. Barbara, Michette, and Ivanka managed to keep their footing, but when the ship didn't right itself, a hush fell over the crowd and the music stopped. The force didn't feel like harsh waters nor a storm, but something sourced from the host-beast itself.

Chloe approach from the hostess station, leaned over and whispered to me.

"Do you think this is a shortage in The Leonardo?"

"If it stops the [REDACTED] feed, we'd be pretty screwed if F4 wakes up."

The frantic lights dimmed and petered out a little. A murmur spread through the crowd as the lights came back up. The guards had positioned themselves evenly around the perimeter of the casino, poised and tense. I didn't want them firing their weapons in here. A bullet could have shattered the far window and drowned us all with F4's cloverblood.

The largest window gave view to an aquarium of

opaque cryptidae that swam aimlessly through F4's insides. Microflora and globular cell-clusters loosened from its digestive tract bounce off larger, darker worm-like bacteria I didn't remember seeing before. We had to be careful what we'd fed the beast through the intravenous tubes of The Leonardo. None of it was FDA-approved, and it would take just the wrong thing to wake the monster up from its sleep. Then we'd have all been right fucked.

A subsonic, doom-metal grumbling rose then through the floor and the dancing lights flickered again. The soundwaves caused the walls to grind inward on their rusted hinges, then they swung back.

The list increased to starboard even further and the murmur increased. I stumbled into one of the waitresses and the tray of drinks she was carrying went flying. A putrid odor rose from the far end of the casino. I was suddenly overwhelmed with lust and want and need and HUNGER. I couldn't pry myself from the thought of Laura on her knees gagging on my cock, eyes aghado as Chloe demolished my ass. I was so deep in my reverie that I scarcely registered a patron doubling over wracked by hacking coughs until he vomited forth a serpentine wave comprised of oily black paste. Transfixed, I waved away the event convincing myself it was somebody's smuggled pet as it formed a mockery of a head and arms that reached out and undulated toward the onlookers who had taken a big step back.

The chain reaction was swift and brutal. The black slime leapt onto the face of a bystander prying open her mouth and sliding down her throat in spite of muffled protests and scrabbling hands desperately trying to pull it away. Shortly after it made egress into her throat, her body began to undulate and twist as she frantically screamed and clawed at her mouth until, with a final sickening shudder, her face exploded spewing forth more of the obsidian serpentine jets.

Rather than screaming and fleeing, an eerie calm settled over the room as many of the passengers—led by Barbara, Michette, and Ivanka—began something between a spiral dance and an orgy as their flesh began blurring together into amorphous masses of sweat slicked roiling flesh radiating need. The undercurrent of lust dragged me with all the urgency of a fish hook through the urethra towards the confusion of twisting flesh—now sprouting beaks, eyes, claws and tentacles. I scarcely noticed how the guards seemed completely indifferent to the spectacle, I was so completely drawn towards the carousel like motion conjoining flesh and need. That is, until one of the passengers—seemingly unfazed by any of the happenings—let forth a blood-curdling howl that seemed to spread through the room affixing attention on her as her face burst apart into a confusion of jagged, uneven fangs encircling a wildly probing radula. Others took up the howl and were swiftly becoming an unnerving mess of teeth and claws as what remained of her face focused its attention towards me and she charged me. Two sharp pops shattered my trance as what was left of the charging woman's head exploded.

I then realized Chloe was standing beside me her Sig Sauer leveled at the pulsating messes scrabbling, clawing, fucking and biting their way across the casino floor. Laura, Jaden, the cop and Old Navy lady were cowering and shaking behind the bar, shell-shocked by what they were witnessing.

"We need to get the fuck out of here" Chloe stated calmly "and we need to make sure whatever the *fuck* this mess is doesn't follow us"

Jaden unlatched the ice station passageway, and one after another, the five of us slid down towards the pancreas of our host-beast. Chloe entered last the rapid pops from her pistol, giving some indication of how much attention we had drawn.

/04/

I turned to the others, partly to take stock of who else from the casino had acted quickly enough to follow us into the gangway, but also to make sure that weird spiral creature of my barmaids hadn't followed us. The emergency lighting was still on but it was still hard to see anything with all the smoke. The ship had righted itself a little but we still had to hold on to the railing to keep our balance.

I told Jaden to come up.

"You know the ship, do you?"

The kid looked at his sister and flashed her one of those same snotty little faces.

"Sure, I told you I've been through every duct," he shrugged. "And this is our third trip on The Finasteride."

The ship angled again to starboard with a jerk, shoving Old Navy lady against the far side of the hallway where she landed hard. She squealed with the impact. I told her to keep her fuckin' voice down.

I looked around. The ducts, although lower and more narrow, weren't all that different from the main hallways of the ship, except that they were slightly more of a marriage between the beast's flesh and the dura-steel lattice of The Finasteride. Veiny and scaled, the brown-crimson membranes of F4 twitched and breathed while constrained by the preset web of metal pipes and harnesses. I'd never been this deep through the monster's insides, but they didn't smell too great. There were also less windows, but when we say through them into the aquarium of the beast's inner world, there was a darker, more subdued wonder to the miracle of what this whole place was.

And yet I knew we were all in big fuckin' trouble, and for the first time, I missed the mainland.

"We need to get to the main deck," I told him. "I need to make sure Brock sent a distress signal."

"What good is that gonna do us here, tranny?" from the cop. "For all we know, the captain's been had for dinner by one of those *things*. And who put *you* in charge, anyway?"

"Me," Chloe said. "Just shut your pie-hole and let's get out of here."

I ignored the cop—he didn't have a gun on him so he was going to be useless, anyway.

"Can you get us there safely?" I asked the kid.

"Sure," he said. "But I mean, it'd be slow."

Old Navy rubbed her arm, but she seemed okay as she shimmied back up to us.

"Shouldn't we try to get weapons?" she asked.

"I don't see what good weapons are against those things."

"The weapons are stockpiled under The Leonardo," Chloe said. "And we might not have access to them.

Plus, it's in the opposite direction."

I told them we just needed to get moving, one way or the other.

"I'm going to Brock, and I'm going to find my sister. That's where she said she'd be."

Even though the vessel felt unstable as fuck, it was still going at an amazing clip, as if we had a flame jet held up to the fuck-beast's anus, propelling us toward Miami in a fraction of the normal time. The effect was disorienting and we all looked at each other to make sure we were really sensing the same thing.

"If this is how Brock's driving," from Laura, "are you sure you want to go up there?"

I remembered the meeting and that whatever had taken place in the casino, he'd had to have some role in making that happen.

"Look, you all do what you want," I said. "I'm going to Brock because you know why? He probably has my sister there."

"All right, then," smiled smug, little Jaden. "Follow me."

We crept along the railing, struggling to keep our grip with the oblique gravity working against us, where up was down, and safety just more danger. I knew what we were getting into, but I had to get to Roz.

More crashing ruin and a weird lime-colored gas plumed from the membrane walls. The smell made us sick and although we didn't want to stop to breathe more of it, it froze us in our tracks. Old Navy was rubbing her injured arm and we held our shirts and skirts up to our faces and squinted.

Old Navy started mewing pathetically about how

much pain she was in.

"It serves you right—ordering a Shirley Temple without a fucking cherry."

"Calm the fuck down, we're almost there" Jaden muttered.

Old Navy began a pithy rejoinder but it was cut off with a low guttural sound followed closely by her mouth vomiting forth cilia alongside her defense for her disgraceful cocktail choice. Her skin trembled as her ribs cracked themselves open and bent into blade sharp appendages webbed with moth-like wings. Her eyes glimmered with smoldering anger as her runny guts fell to the floor and her knees buckled before readjusting themselves to bend backwards. She tensed herself about to spring from her cricket like haunches when a stream of bullets tore her face apart leaving her gasping through her malformed mouth on the floor, blood and ichor polling around her. Quintal strode in from the gloom, flanked by six of his security guards and planted his boot on the remains of Old Navy's shattered face before emptying the magazine into her twitching, shitfucked body.

"I'll bet you and your faggot friends are glad to see me," he sneered. "Now, if you don't want to end up a fucked apart mess like your friend, you'll come with me; the Captain has use for you."

/05/

The guards led us single file down a jagged, irregular slope toward the Captain's deck. Quintal held his pulse-rifle to the back of Chloe's head. I couldn't see her face but I knew she had to be thinking of some way to get the gun away from him. I wasn't even going to try—there were too many of them, and I wanted to know what was really going on. I had to hear it from Brock himself, even though I knew where Quintal's ambitions lay and that we weren't going to find much for safety in the control room.

The ship groaned louder, and I heard this underlying hissing that didn't sound like anything mechanical. It sounded like it was coming from behind the walls of membrane. At one point, there was a steady grating that resonated in my prick. It subsided after a moment, but I knew we had to find a way out of there before we succumbed to the madness that was engulfing the ship.

"It's the F4," Laura whispered. "The [REDACTED] must totally be wearing off."

"We're in big trouble if it wakes up, aren't we?"

"You might." Quintal giggled ominously.

"I need to find Roz," I said. "I'm not leaving without her."

Quintal glanced back at us, and squinted.

"Just shut the fuck up," he said. "I told you, Carol. Your sister's with Brock. He'll explain everything for you."

"I think we know enough," from the pig, who was chaperoned at the rear of our procession. He didn't seem to be taking the loss of Old Navy well at all. I hadn't seen them together before that night, but who knows if they'd only just met and decided they were soul-mates.

I was surprised Chloe hadn't said anything. I don't she wanted to call much attention herself, though. Usually I can read her well, but Quintal had separated us for a reason.

Just as we entered the entry suite for Brock's chambers, another explosion sounded at the back of the vessel. The concussion was smaller than the others but the frequency between them was pulling us tighter. We were in one hell of a fuckstorm, and riding on the back of the last surviving kaiju we knew of on earth. There was more to this than just us.

Quintal stepped forward and slid the main doors open. The smell hit us like a battering ram. A combination of henna paste, bad milk, swamp decay, and vanilla. Once the Chernobyl-colored cloud passed and we recovered a little, we stepped forward into Brock's chamber.

The ambience in there was stuffy, and what little light there was came from beneath the ground. Quintal gestured with his rifle for us to go all the way in, but I had this child's fear of the deep end. But this was much more than that—even with everything going on all around us, we were walking into a sewer.

Once Chloe, and then I stepped over the threshold, the sound became muffled but it was easier to see. Brock swiveled his chair around, working against his green-grey fleshrolls that spilled over the edges of his uniform, and he beamed at us in his new-fangled glory. Sea anemone-like protrusions pulsed on his face, leaking thick yellow mucus that helped lend the room its special odor. His ibex-horns spiraled out from his head with an ever-steady progress, curling in on themselves when they needed balance and subtlety. His inchoate tentacles squired and grasped the sides of his chair.

Just behind The Captain stood my sister Roz. Some guard was holding a straight razor against her throat. Brock then grabbed her wrist and sucked at the inside of her wrist. His ibex-horns grew even for with every influx of her blood, as did his tentacles. My sister looked sheet-white from the experience she was having. Her eyes were full moons.

"Go and greet your Captain, you stupid trap bitch," Quintal exclaimed with sadistic glee, pushing the barrel of his pulse rifle into my back.

Chloe and I stepped up together. She looked worried for the first time I'd ever seen her. I just felt pissed off that I'd let ourselves be suckered into something like this.

The walls were full of bruised, crusty spirals, sucking all manner of dust and sweat droplets into their little anuses.

But Captain Brock and my sister Roz were the main attraction.

"Carol!" enthused Brock the squid-goat, taking a little break from sucking Roz's blood, "so nice of you to finally join us!"

The nasty, lopsided energy in the room concentrated in the wall directly behind Brock's swivel chair, a deep vortex of lavender cirrus clouds that swirled in opposite directions. Dark, slimy tendrils writhed out at us from deep inside the portal, confused blind penises in search of a helper. We were being invited to a party we wanted nothing to do with. Something told me no distress signal had been sent, so I didn't even ask.

The Captain didn't even seem to register Chloe's presence.

I stepped forward.

"Let her go, assholes."

Brock only clamped his mouth back onto Roz's wrist and drank harder.

"Get the fuck off her!"

I rushed at them, but Quintal squashed my hasty plan by planting the stock of his pulse rifle hard into my kidney.

"Show the Captain your respect," Quintal grinned. "You'll be punished for insubordination."

"By that you mean no big pay-raise from Regalia Corporate, right?" I shot back.

Brock shoved my sister away. She fell onto the dura-steel floor. I tried to rise from my knees but Quintal smashed the butt of his rifle into my temple, dropping me to my knees again.

"Bring the trannies forward," Brock commanded, his mouth salivating with sadistic delight.

Chloe stepped up beside me. Laura joined us without hesitation. I glanced at her and she shrugged, gave me the nod. My trans-dar had been well-tuned, after all.

"We're not going to Miami," Laura said first, addressing Brock. "We're never docking there, we're going somewhere else entirely, aren't we?"

Brock leaned towards us, his sweat pouring off his bulging forehead in a waterfall. His tentacles rubbed together, scheming in all pettiness.

"He's taking us into the Hex-Waters," said Chloe.

"FUCK YES!" the Captain roared.

"We're there already," Roz muttered, lifting her head a little from the floor.

"Three-cherry slot machine score, you fuckin' shemale trap-fags," Quintal sneered.

"Listen, Quintal," Brock began, trying to sound magnanimous with that haughty, mutated voice of his. "We could use some positivity here. After all, think of what Carol's going to do for us. It's to *your* benefit also, remember?"

"I'll believe it when I see it."

"This is only the beginning."

Brock came down from his throne and slithered over to us. His skin was mottling and clumps of his hair fell out like pulled daisies. A few crab-dogs hovered at his heels, licking the fetid air.

"What do you think you're going to prove with the Hex Zone?" I asked him, even as he became more of an *it* with each passing moment. "We're never going to be seen again."

"The Hex isn't our destination, it's only the route. Actually only the first leg of the journey."

"So where the fuck are you taking us?"

"Kutada!"

I looked at Chloe.

Brock brightened at Laura.

"Go ahead, Miss Palmer," he said. "Fill Miss Stratham and Miss Flanagan in on this adventure. You're the resident expert here."

"Kutada's the Sorcerer of Kolkhorst Atoll," she told us. "It's a hundred nautical miles east of Bora Bora. They say he's the one who originally summoned the Fuck-beasts from the depths."

"All four of them," Brock offered.

"Who is *they*?"

"Just *they*."

"What, why are you taking us northeast, then?" I asked. "Kolkhorst's in the goddamn Pacific!"

"It's not on any of the charts, Carol," from Laura. "There's no way to reach it from the water. You can only get to it through The Sway."

Brock's tentacles extended, writhed at the word then spoken aloud, like it was a candied invocation.

"What the fuck's a Sway?"

"The End of the earth," Laura sighed, looking down.

By then, Roz had struggled to her feet. She still looked weak from loss of blood. I wanted to go to her but Quintal kept his gun aimed at me. I flipped him the bird and stepped forward anyway, sidestepping Brock who tried to trip me with one of his appendages but I just hopped right over that.

I took my sister by her forearm and brought her over to the others.

"The True Power of The Sway," Brock told us, "is in our host. F4 is the last surviving Fuck-beast, and we're bringing it back to Kutada. But what he doesn't expect is that we already have the key to unleashing that power."

"You're the captain of the ship," I said. "What more power do you need?"

"Well, we can't all be celebrities like *you*," Brock said. "And I've been sucking on Regalia's tits for too many years, riding this same cruise for two solid years, back-and-forth. It's my turn to take what's mine."

"You're off to a great start," Chloe said.

I realized why Brock had tried to keep us distracted with the casino. He'd also stationed Quintal there to rein us in, trap us in there when we reached The Hex. But no one had counted on Jaden knowing hidden egress points of The Finasteride, nor of Laura's knowledge of the Fuck-beast. F4, the last of its kind.

"Tell them the good part," Quintal enthused.

"Of course!" The Captain snapped. His jaw hit the floor due in part to his new gelatinous anatomical capabilities. "It's time to unleash The Sway. And then we awaken the mind Fuck-beast Four. And then its power is mine. For that task we need a rebis, but those are in short supply; thankfully we can use a tranny like you."

And at that, a bus-sized ochre hand darted forth from the vortex behind Brock. It was covered in brown fur and worms. A huge blast of hyperkinetic wind hit everyone and sent us flying back into each other. The hand grabbed Brock by the waist, and pulled him back into the vortex. Quintal was blown off his feet and pinned against the far wall. He blindly fired his machine gun and everyone but his guards ducked—dispatching four of his own men with clean headshots. The force of the winds blew their splattered brains into our faces and mouths combining the gross gelatinous feel of spongy brain matter with the coppery taste of blood—I didn't even hesitate grabbing Roz by the wrist and dragging her away from the portal.

I think Laura expected this split-second opportunity to arrive at some point, and to her credit, she sprang into it and as if she could tell where we would be blown by the force of The Sway, corralling us toward the main entrance. She even helped the cop, for reasons I cannot fully understand.

I slammed the main doors behind us even as they bulged with pus and blood.

/06/

Right as we started tear-assing down the corridor, another huge convulsion tore through The Finasteride. A huge, subsonic moan crackled over the PA speakers, and we weren't sure if the sound was human. We didn't care to go back and investigate.

The emergency lights strobed intermittently, and the membrane walls of the Fury-beast yellowed, like a sick dog's tongue. I heard gunfire erupting behind us, and it seemed far, but not far enough. They would be coming.

I looked back for a second and saw the cop was struggling to keep up. But I wasn't going to slow down. I wasn't sure right then, but the cop was clutching his stomach as if about to puke something up.

Roz had to shove me from behind a few times because my prick was slowing me down. I'd worked so hard 24/7 to get that fucker imprisoned but there it was, giving me shit and getting hard without any hot thoughts to spur it. I didn't know what it was happening, but I figured it was just the adrenaline. It felt like it was being inflated by some spectral bicycle pump. The pain began to throb and fill my head with flash-fantasies of blowing myself just to get it to pipe down, already. The dysphoria was bad enough, but running bow-legged like some slapstick comedy sketch was pissing me off.

"LOOK OUT!"

Chloe was a few yards ahead of us, pointing in our direction. Laura looked back and her mouth opened to scream.

An ebony wave streaked with snot and intestines spanned every inch of the corridor about ten feet behind us, traveling at a hungry pace.

It had the face of the cop and its eyes were green suns.

"Um, let's get the fuck out of here?"

We reached Chloe, Laura, and Jaden and bounded up the nearest stairway. As the list increased to port again we had to cling to the railing. Gravity was working against us, but that didn't slow the cop slime monster down any.

But I felt a different threat from the thing—that it didn't want to eat me or transform me over into of its little helpers, but that it wanted to *take me* back to the mainland, to the nightmare, to the media fuck who had made my life hell.

There was unfinished business.

And that terrified me far worse, but it electrified my being and I took my sister by the elbow, and we flew up the stairs in just a few desperate leaps.

We reached the upper level and there was no door to put between us and our pursuer. My dick hurt so badly, it's like it was slithering down my right leg and I expected it to reach my shoe at any moment. I wanted to snap it off and use it as a bludgeon against the cop slime monster, my rage against the prick lent fury to our pursuer.

Another moan sounded in the walls.

Jaden took the lead.

"Let's go for the vent!" the kid said, pointing at a maintenance sign that just barely concealed a heating duct. It would slow our progress but we had to get out of sight. There was a chance, at least.

"Okay, GO!"

Then Brock's deep, gurgling voice came over the crackling PA system:

Yes! The vent! The vent! Go for the vent, Carol! The Vent!

We ignored his taunting and scrambled along with the cop beast-thing at our heels.

The escape route was darker but its plastic walls made it easier to see the inner workings of the Fury-beast's lungs. It was breathing more rapidly, as if in the throes of a wet dream. We ran at a crouch, and we had to keep up with Jaden who was of course shorter than us by half. The ground was more level but my groin had ballooned by then. I had to improvise this sort of shuffle-bounce motion that at least kept my forward momentum.

Jaden grabbed onto his sister's hand and led us along the beast's ribcage. We were going to the outer levels. I looked behind us and didn't see the slime creature.

We turned a corner and found the way blocked by debris.

Brock's voice again:

See what I did there? That's only half of what I have for you!

The kid didn't miss a beat. He backtracked to a

tight junction and led us down a narrower passageway.

Chloe slowed down and when I caught up she whispered to me, "I don't know what good weapons are going to be against those things."

"I don't think we have much choice. We have to get away."

"We have to take the ship."

"And go *where*?"

She looked down at her feet. Usually Chloe never shut the fuck up once she got an idea in her head. But this time she had no brilliant plan.

Then she asked me why I thought Brock had me singled out. I looked at Roz.

"Did he tell you anything back there?" I asked her. "Before he started—"

Her wrist still had an oval of cigar-tip-sized punctures where Brock had left them when drinking her blood.

"Let's just keep moving, okay?" Roz sighed. "I'll try to tell you once we find somewhere to hide."

"Brock unleashed The Sway," Chloe said. "I don't think there's anywhere safe to hide now."

We turned a corner and the only one we saw was Laura, silhouetted in front of a large porthole. She told us Jaden had found a way up to The Leonardo, but we had to climb up the side of the huge supply shaft. I looked down through the hole. About fifty feet down was a boiling mass of dark water.

I looked up. Jaden was hanging onto a steel utility ladder built into the side of the shaft.

"Hey kid!" I called to him. "No fuckin' way! Get back here!"

"Do you want to get to The Leonardo or not?" he answered. I wanted to slap the little fucker but he was right. There was no other way out of there.

Brock taunted over the speakers again:

Yes! The shaft! Climb the shaft! It's the only way to The Leonardo!

The stream from below gnawed at the skin and within seconds my clothes were stuck to me. Chloe went up the ladder after Jaden, then me, then Laura. She insisted on going last. I liked her more with each leg of this little adventure.

The steel rungs of the ladder were hot from the steam so I tried using my sleeves. I yelled at everyone to hurry, because I didn't want another convulsion to dislodge us into that pool. Hell only knew what was waiting down there.

I saw no sign of the cop monster, but I also figured it was just playing with us. Maybe it only wanted its PBR and pretzel rolls.

We were halfway up when a new, angst-ridden moan shook the shaft, the acoustics made it sound much closer than it had out in the halls. The ship also teetered over about 30 degrees again, this time to starboard. We had to hold on and Chloe lost one of her Louboutins into the soup. She cursed. I did, too, the fuckin' shoe hit me in the face during its descent.

Laura hissed at me to keep going. I think she had a fear of heights, but there was plenty else to fear all around us. I remember thinking we were just postponing the inevitable. While that was likely the case, I wanted to get Roz away from Brock, at least. I didn't want to let that fuck have her in his clutches again. She hadn't fully recovered by this time. I think extreme terror was driving her.

There was a bright light near the top, breaking through the stream clouds. Jaden gestured toward it, and I steeled myself because it looked like Roz was faltering. I should have asked Chloe to let her go first.

We were almost there when another convulsion raged through the ship. This time it fucked with us—it was like we had been sideswiped. Chloe's grip failed her and she paused just a moment when she tried to recover before she tumbled back in the air and fell past us screaming into the black water.

/07/

"**M**otherfucker!"

We'd escaped from the shaft and the ship returned to level. We sheltered on a metal grate where the steam still got at us but it wasn't as intense. I knew I couldn't go down after her and I was pissed at myself for getting her to come with me. If she'd stayed with Brock at least Chloe would still be alive.

Laura tried to console me. Chloe's work before this nightmare had meant a great deal to her, also, she'd said to me one time at the bar, but her interest had been more academic. Every other scholar she had known had transitioned at one point or another, and her lectures and talk show appearances had been proof-positive of what was possible. She was the worst of trans misogyny.

Sure, Chloe was a selfish cunt. I felt she'd earned her sash, though. She'd been on the frontlines of the culture war, whereas I'd only been one of its lame-ass casualties. Chloe had fucked the religious right up the ass with her gifts and strengths. I mean, who doesn't have flaws?

Even Jaden wasn't having any luck consoling me, though. I was screaming my lungs out, mostly out of anger that Brock and Quintal had us running from their own pathetic quest for power. Like their authority wasn't enough, they had to fuck the employees over, as well.

It's all such a familiar pattern.

Never enough power.

Makes one wonder if cis dudes just have a complex with their manhood, their pricks aren't big enough so they just need more supremacy to make sure no one else takes their spot. It's a joke that we all pay for with our fuckin' lives.

"She knew how to hack into The Leonardo!" I told them. "We're fucked now! Why bother going any further, it's just going to be more of this bullshit."

"Look, Chloe," my sister said, grabbing me by the shoulders. "She hacked into it only *twice*, what makes you think she was going to be able to again? Brock said he knew all about that shit, and he probably set new codes. So just shut up about her, she fucked you over repeatedly!"

"You just hate her because I look up to her."

"No, I hate her because she treated you like a sap. Those sex videos were only intended to shore up her clickbait. You know this is how The Ratites found you again, too, right?"

The floor screeched with new violence and we almost fell back into the shaft. Laura braced against it just in time.

"I can try to get us access to the antenna," she shouted at us. "Let's just get the fuck over there and see if we can get help!"

The air started to smell like all the toilets on board had exploded.

Roz and Laura grabbed me by both elbows and Jaden

led us again. I wondered how he knew these innards of the ship so well, like had he willingly crawled up that shaft before? I hadn't even known this part of the ship existed, but then we were inside the belly of the beast, one doesn't think too much about tech shit while you're there, you just want to make it through the day.

The kid had trouble opening the door. The noise around us kept growing louder and that put some fire in us. Me, Roz, and Laura went up to help him shove against it, but it wouldn't budge.

I picked up a crowbar.

It was a huge mistake, but that's how miracles happen.

The winds were the first thing.

The air cut us. The ocean was gone. The Finasteride floated on a seething layer of blood that bubbled with erect kielbasa.

The sky was a combination of bruises and snot.

A thick phalanx of crab-dogs greeted us and charged. A few stragglers at the front had been blowing each other but then took a break when we interrupted their party. Live and let live, right?

We hadn't ever seen the crab-dogs as a potential threat. They were just a waste product of the Fury-beast, just dandruff. But the rules had changed. The universe was upside down.

But the antenna was right there. The lava lamp blobs traipsing through the skies hadn't affected it. The Leonardo stood about a hundred feet above deck, and there were several utility apartments at its base. If we could get inside, we stood a decent chance at fortifying ourselves while we summoned whatever help there was.

I wondered if The Sway had a coast guard.

"Just go!" Roz shouted.

The creatures attacked Jaden first. I fought some of them off with the crowbar, splitting their orange flesh and splintering their vertebrae. They let out a collective howl as we fought our way forward.

I thought about Sigmund for the first time in a while. I missed him, despite everything that had happened with us. My regret didn't slow me down, it made more violent—I kept thinking every parasite I brained was one of The Ratite Cult that had made my life such a living hell.

I don't know how, but the horde sensed and latched onto my trauma. The shitheads backed off from Jaden, Laura, and Roz and I kept swinging the pipe at them as they chomped at me. It was just enough of a chance for the others to evade them and get to the entrance.

One of the crab-dogs was halfway in which prevented us from getting the metal door all the way shut. The little fucker squealed to its brethren and tried to dislodge itself, biting at our shins all the while. Roz kicked it in the face. Laura and I slammed our bodies repeatedly against the door, and we split the monster in two after a minute or so. It kept screaming even after it lost its lower half to the chaos raging outside.

I was so pissed off, I finally crowbarred its head in. Laura's eyes went wide, I don't think she knew I had that much ferocity. But losing Chloe in the shaft had unleashed something in me, and maybe that's why The Sway was engulfing us, like it was feeding off my anger and hate. We'd been betrayed by the same people who'd been responsible for our safety, and their powerlust had fucked everything up. I didn't have to accept that shit from the dickfaces anymore, so I was going to get us the fuck out of there come hell or high water.

"Let's get to the main stairs!" Jaden shouted as the crab-dogs assaulted the door. I didn't want them to gain entry, so I told everyone to try and find something we could prop against the door. Roz came back with a metal folding chair and we wedged it beneath the door handle. We figured it would hold.

The area was dark and mostly bare except for some discarded power cells that looked more like dildos. My erection had calmed down a bit, so it was easier to walk as Jaden led us down the long corridor.

We'd only gone a few yards when we heard a sloughing sound behind us.

"Umm, guys?"

Jaden stopped and we looked back. A black puddle was spreading from beneath the door. Even as it grew, the liquid gathered itself at the middle-front into a solid column of goop. Three bulbous, glowing-red eyes then emerged from inside the material, dancing with each other in a clockwise pattern as if trying to decide what to do, finally settling for a vertical grid that reminded me of a traffic light, but the only color was red, but there was no fucking way we were going to sit still for whatever it had planned for us. Then it spread outwards into a more seemingly human, pro-wrestler shape as if trying to creatively interpret our own semblance of species.

Its mouth then opened huge, splitting its belly into a widening, drooling orifice.

"Be my friend?" it said in a sexless, gurgling voice as it formed and rose upon about a dozen short, writhing legs that then sprouted hundreds of desperate penises. Every new member it sprouted consisted of the same creamy black substance.

We turned and ran. The main stairs glinted just past the flickering emergency lights, it seemed pretty far but we weren't sticking around to get sticky with the friendly monster.

"It looks like someone knows the ship better than you, Jaden!"

"Fuck you," he called back. That made me smile a little. That was what I needed to hear to start liking the kid a little.

Roz started to flag behind, grunting and reaching forward. I shifted so I could prod her along from behind. I made the mistake of looking back at the creature.

The thing was coming after us with an ophidian rippling, and with a momentum that gave it the appearance of a tsunami. It puckered its mouth like a fish, and it grew exponentially as it gained on us. But that was just the teaser trailer—behind the monster, glowing with purple and green swirly gases, came The Sway, hungry as its incipient pet.

We took the stairs like, two or three at a time. The railing made it easier to ascend, even though the grip felt clammy and cold.

I shouted at them to not look back. That had been a serious fuckup on my part. I think it sensed something in me that magnetized The Sway to my asshole.

I'd never been inside The Leonardo but remembered this much about it: in addition to delivering the sedatives and wet dreams intravenously into our F4 Fury-beast host, it was also a direct-link to the extra-stellar broadcast satellites of Regalia Corp. Even though we were obviously in the far reaches of The Hex Waters, The Sway had not taken The Finasteride entirely. So, I knew there might still be a chance to at least zero onto us. We could always ask them to blast us out of the ocean. It would be quick.

Jaden reached the top of the stairway and waved us along. Then he looked back like a little jackoff and shouted for us to run faster. The slime creature used the metal framework of the facility to its advantage. Its main bulk couldn't move as fast as us, but its tendrils extended far along with a crazy anti-gravity force and was trying to surround us on both railings and hug us back to the main bulk. I wasn't going to let happen. Brock had already fucked my sister up, and his treachery had taken Chloe away. So using my body weight I swung the crowbar against the railing in an attempt to stay the progress of the slime. But for every bit that splatted and fell away, the limb grew back instantaneously.

We got to the level. I hoped Jaden knew what the fuck he was doing. Laura rushed up to him and whispered something I didn't catch.

"Hurry!" I screamed at Roz. Our slime friend had generated a massive tongue and was licking at the back of my sister's head. I grabbed her hand and pulled. She screamed in pain and I realized too late I'd hurt her shoulder.

I fuck everything up.

But she's still my sister so I was going to help her get out of there. I held the crowbar, stepped down in front of Roz, and approached the creature and The Sway.

They both engulfed me in a SINGLE BITE.

PART TWO

/01/

As I sat in the waiting area, my left index finger kept going up to a single, stray hair on the middle of my jaw. I'd been trying to ignore it all morning, but that was like trying to keep your tongue from massaging an aching tooth.

The fucker wasn't that long, just a couple of centimeters out, but it felt thick and stark. I knew I was probably the only one who would notice it, but I also knew it wasn't going to be distracting and as the anxiety consumed me in the courtroom, I'd be constantly invalidated. My testimony alone was already being contested both by defense lawyers and the media.

The crusade against me online was something else entirely. I had that much to look forward to, but I wanted to get that shit day over with. I'd been through more than my share of harassment, already. I'd only wanted to do the right thing and tell the police what I'd seen happen. But everyone just ended up turning against me, just for putting myself out there.

I'd longed for my tweezers. I could kill that little

fuck. Shit, that's what I'd wanted life to be like—when something sucks for you just pluck it out, scrutinize it for a moment, consider its worth to you, then judge accordingly, and flick it away just like any and all trash.

But I was stuck in some shit I couldn't control so easily. And I didn't know that I was going to be the one in serious trouble. That's the price you pay for doing the right thing.

The court officer feathered the door open and called me in, looking at the floor all the while, ashamed to be breathing the same air as me.

I shrugged and checked myself in the two-way mirror at the far end of the waiting room. This was the third day of testimony and I'd done my best to try and look assimilated. But there was no way to be good enough for that.

As I walked in, a hush fell over the court gallery again, a few cis coughs towards the back, like always. I knew what to expect there. It was their problem, not mine.

"Can you state your name for the record?"

This was Teemer once again, the defense attorney for John Wilkes Booth (funny name for a kid)—this was the dude who'd driven the car, used the victim's iPhone, and got nailed. He kept watching me from the defense table, making little stabbing gestures with his ballpoint pen. I wasn't afraid of that fucker.

"Carol Stratham."

Everyone in the country knew who I was by then.

"Have you always gone by that name?"

My mouth opened as the prosecutor sprang out of his chair.

"Objection, your honor, my God!"

"Have you always had a dumb-sounding name?" I shot back at Teemer. "One that sounds like it belongs to a television clown?"

But they saw *me* as the sideshow.

Judge Millikin chimed in, exasperated.

"Objection sustained."

I looked over at the jury, so impartial and full of civic duty. A couple of the mothers wouldn't look at me for more than a few seconds.

I thought I'd looked just fine.

The prosecutor, a lovely brunette woman named Tendean, moved to strike the question from the record and the judge complied.

"Your honor this has to do with calling the witness's honesty into question."

"The former name of the witness has no bearing on this case. According to the transcript Miss—Stratham has had that name for—"

"Two years," I told them. "Christ, do we have to go through this again? Do you want to know who killed Mr. Fuller or not?"

"Examination will continue as part of due process," said Teemer.

"Defense would be advised to stick with a relevant line of inquiry."

The judge was decent enough, I figured. But I was getting really bored by that whole experience. It's not like you see on television. "Fantastic," Teemer sneered. "Let's go over the events of that night of August 27."

"Yeah sure, why not? You seem to like the story."

/02/

Sigmund and I had both settled in in Wilmington, North Carolina. His band was called The Four Fucks even though there were only three people in it. Sig played bass with these other two jackholes Andrew on guitar and sort-of-vokills and Jamison on drums. They all lived in this shitty ranch house in a cul-de-sac a few miles from the city limits. I stayed in town because I wanted to be closer to the restaurant where I had bartended. I hadn't found any library or archives work and took what I could get. Also, I was passing well enough by then, for people who hadn't bothered looking at me twice.

I got the call one night as I was closing and had thrown the last drunk home to his wife's tits. It was Sigmund on Caller ID, so I figured it had to be weed he wanted me to pick up for him on my way over to The Four Fucks house. But it turned out to be way more frivolous than that.

Sig sounded like he'd finally had enough of his band situation. I'd ceased to talk to him about it. I knew how much this had meant to him, but after I'd moved down closer to him that was all he ever talked about.

"Jamison took the van," he said. "And now he ran out of gas and he's stuck just outside of Raleigh."

"What? Good," I told him. "Let him sit there and rot."

Jamison was the one who gave me the most shit, behind my back most of the time. Always the drummer. Whatever, he always feathered the snare, which made the band sound weak.

I guess there'd been some sort of huge noisefest up in Akron. The Four Fucks had been invited to co-headline but none of them had enough gas money to get all the way up there and back.

Sig told me they'd all been sitting in their living room watching TV and suddenly Jamison had darted up from their tatty couch.

"You're all pussies!" he said to his band-housemates. "I'm in a band with a bunch o'pussies! Just like King Fag's tranny over there up his ass!"

Sig said he stood up for me but I doubt it because he never did, usually. At least not when Jamison said anything to my face. I usually the one to tell him to go fuck his mother.

"I'm going to Ohio without ya," Jamison had told them as he walked away. "I'm going to play the show still, so fuck ya!"

He never brought his drums, he just drunk-drove the van away from their house, leaving a cloud of empties behind him.

"Maybe you all need to start drinking Natural Ice again, instead," I told him. "You'd have gas money to play shows. I can't give you a ride every time."

"We need the van, though."

"None of you has Triple-A or anything?"

"We don't have shit."

"Christ, Sig," I told him. I just worked a double and I have to work tomorrow, too."

He didn't answer right away.

"Besides, wouldn't it be better to just let him wait there until tomorrow, might sober him up?"

"I promise I'll make it up to you."

That was Sig's pet phrase of late. But it worked on me. It works on a lot of us when we feel undesirable in the world.

I looked around the bar, it was calm and dark. I wasn't sure where my life was anymore. Neither one of my parents ever had the chance to know I'd transitioned because they were still missing somewhere out there in the ocean, and I was band mom to a bunch of unemployed delinquents. Sig and I were in love back then. That was why I put up with that shit. He was my first boyfriend, and it was a big deal to me.

But I still wonder why I let it happen.

/03/

I'll readily admit I was a complain-ey bitch as we made our way north in my Honda Civic. It was at least two hours to Raleigh, and I'm surprised Jamison made it even that far. I also wondered if he'd killed anyone on the way. By all accounts he'd been pretty fuckin' drunk when he took the van.

"Look," I told Sigmund. "It's just really telling for me that you're so quick to enlist my help in picking up your stupid drummer and you don't even fuck me anymore."

Andrew was sitting in the back seat. I said that in front of him on purpose. I knew he'd been raised Baptist, so I wanted to ram my trans prick down his throat, since Andrew looked like he could give fellatio like a chocolate lab/pit mix looking to lap up a glut of peanut butter from a rubber kong toy. Sure, he was usually quiet but I know he'd played right along with Jamison when they used my photograph as a dartboard. I saw it up there. So, I dished what I could *when* I could. I want that again, without having to eat so much pigshit.

F4

"Can we stop for cigarettes, Carol?" Andrew asked.

"You said the fourth fuck is at a rest stop. They might have something there."

"I gotta take a squirt," he muttered.

"God commands it," I told them. "Fine, just shut your dick holes and let me drive, get this over with. Make sure you use the right bathroom."

There was a sign after a few more miles, and I was wanting a coffee anyway. The raw sewage that passes for such things in North Carolina would do me in good enough stead because I knew I needed to be awake and this was going to take us into the dawn.

The rain was coming down harder, covering the windshield with more bullshit. I cranked the wipers and the music, both. I had a mixtape of Florence and the Machine with me so I was trying to play anything that Andrew hated.

I sing-sneered the Deliverance banjo as we pulled off the highway and turned onto a darker road. I couldn't see the gas station in either direction so I just swung a right. All decent people were asleep or fucking their pets and/or their cousins in their homes at that hour. I looked out at the black treetops swaying in the wind and wondered what the rest of my life would be like.

One car passed us going to other way. Its lights were off, but I didn't dare flash my beams at it because I knew urban legends well enough. There were certain fates you never tempt, especially out there in the boondocks. I watched it swerve a little as it receded in the mirror. I wondered how many more of these unfortunates we'd run across before I could go home and try to get an hour's sleep.

We found the gas station after a bend in the road. I don't know why, but I felt super-nervous about something I couldn't place right then. I rubbed the underside of my chin, where the bullshit stubble had returned.

I was like, *Fuck, I have to get out of this place.*

I thought of my sister Roz. She'd been trying to get me to move in with her near Raleigh, so we could deal with the insurance company together. Our parents were still missing somewhere out in the Pacific Ocean, along with 247 others. Even though the flight had been well-documented, the wreckage still hadn't been found, and thus we had no proof.

They'd also said that the cause of the accident was also unprovable.

My parents didn't even know I had transitioned. That was another thing that fucked with me, thinking about them. Roz and I were orphans who just wanted to find some life somewhere on the mainland. That was like asking for the moon's creamy filling.

Shit, the Fury-beasts were proof enough. If the flight my parents were on hadn't been caught in the wake of the Boss Battle they might have made it home and I could've come out to them. But then again, I might never have left New York, despite everything. There were so many things I wanted to go back and change. But too much had happened.

I owed Roz a phone call, but if I was to visit her up in the city I wouldn't make it back in time to open the bar. Fuck everything.

I pulled into the station. It seemed deserted. Once I opened the car door I noticed the rain and wind had picked up hardcore. That gave me a lot of anxiety about my appearance even though I knew I'd have to go in and use my card. At least it had my real name on it.

The dude at the cashier looked like he hadn't slept in weeks. He wore a Pantera shirt and about a decade of smokeless tobacco use. There was a lot more of that down there than I'd seen up north.

Sig came up to me and apologized.

I told him this band mom shit was just getting old. They didn't respect me, anyway. And there I was, buying gas for them.

Something had to change, but I didn't know where to start. New York had been a total wash, but I couldn't go back anyway because it was still trying to rebuild after F4 had leveled half of it.

I wondered if any of the other trans girls had survived the F4 party. I hadn't tried to contact anyone up there. I had enough to deal with, and they hadn't wanted me around, anyway. To contact them would just be another poser intrusion.

"I'll pay you back," Sig whispered to me.

I looked at my boyfriend and felt a newborn coldness. It was like I only existed still to prop him up. The man who had cared about enough to remember my birthday seemed to have gone somewhere else. I mean, I knew he was still in him somewhere but hiding so deep inside I didn't even know where to start looking.

"Okay, what kind again?" I asked him.

"Marlboro Reds?"

I knew all the while but didn't want to dignify that.

I bought them for him and he went outside to smoke them.

I was so tired.

I wished I'd been born in a better time.

So much seemed out of reach.

Fuck.

I was totally stuck and I didn't want to admit it. And this was my third strike: first the egg growing up scared on Nantucket, then the loser in New York, and finally the damaged goods traipsing through the bumfuck south.

If only I knew what was coming up.

An older man walked in, shattering my wonderful trance. He looked sort of familiar but I couldn't place him. His skin shone beautifully olive under the fluorescent lighting. I hadn't seen him at the bar, but maybe it was his eyebrows. They were really grey and bushy, as if he'd grown them with the pride-maintenance of a ZZ Top beard. They were epic, and I knew I'd seen that style somewhere, maybe in a reality TV show. We either pay too much attention to those things, or way too little—so much for balance.

His horn-rimmed glasses were just like mine.

"Pardon me, miss," he said, stepping just past me at the counter. He asked the clerk if they sold any of those mobile phone battery chargers you plug into your cigarette lighter. The clerk stared at him blankly, maybe because he wasn't another white jackoff like me but I saw some right next to the porn behind the counter so I gestured there.

"Thank you, dear," he said. "You're lovely."

I smiled at being called *dear*.

"This storm is a test from God," he said. The clerk didn't even seem to hear him.

I shrugged.

"Test?"

"Of our resilience."

He was so smiley, I wondered if anything ever bothered him. I could drop my pants and test the possibility. God the quiz-master.

"Sure, I guess." I mumbled. "Resilience."

I finished paying for the gas and the portable canister we'd need for the stranded Four Fucks van.

The eyebrow man finished his transaction next and I steeled myself for the wind and the rain and the cold. We still had about an hour's drive ahead of us, not including the return trip.

Another car pulled into the lot. It parked next to a sleek, silver Lexus that stood in nice contrast with my old Honda. Its license plate read "JAM ROD." This other one, a Ford sedan I think. I didn't study the plate. Its lights were off, which was off-putting because the rain was so gnarly. There two white dudes in the front seat. They looked like pretty standard Deliverance stock, and when I see shit like that I don't tend to stick around for deep *getting-to-know-you* conversation. I didn't make eye contact with them, but it definitely looked like the car that had passed us on the road.

I handed the empty canister to Sig and told him to put twenty bucks worth in. I figured that should have been enough for the fuck-van to get back to Wilmington.

/03.1/

The rain and wind were picking up even more and I was trying to see better. I'm not the best night driver, especially on the highway. But I knew I could do better than Jamison. I told Andrew that when we got there to get the van keys from the little fuck and take the wheel, himself.

Sigmund asked me how things were progressing with the insurance company.

"We're getting nowhere," I said. "As far as I know, Roz is in touch with the other families and they're going to try something together."

"Yeah, good luck with that," Andrew said. Sig told him to shut up. I wanted to say the same thing to Sigmund, though, because I didn't want him bringing up my personal shit up in front of his bandmate.

"We can't do anything without death certificates," I said.

"I don't get it," from Sig. "Everyone knows what happened."

I shrugged.

"Just let me drive, okay?"

/04/

F1, the first Fury-beast that anyone knew of, came to San Francisco during the early morning of April 18. This was the whateverth anniversary of the original quake that had leveled the place. Perhaps this was the best way to celebrate. Its emergence from the bay spawned a gigantic tsunami that heralded great things to come that day.

I never saw a photograph of this first beast but I've heard it described as looking most like an axolotl that could stand up on its hind legs. This creature, although it was the hugest in mass, was apparently the most vulnerable to military weapons. Artillery doesn't have much short-term traction against a mountain, but when it lost its arm against the coordinated volley that descended from several fighter jets and the satellite-based Destructor Weapon, it regrew the lost appendage within minutes and continued to lay waste to inland California. Also like some Ambystomatidae, the skin of F1 shifted colors according to its temperament. Many observers thought it was the Father (or mother) of The Sway, because of the gargantuan swirling patterns that would sometimes form around it, cycling like planetary rings. But science could never pin that down. They hadn't been able to get so close to the being as it stomped zip codes into paste, one by one. It finally took a nap when it reached the Sierras.

Then it was Brisbane's turn. F2 came out of the water on April 27, during lunch time. Witnesses reported seeing the huge waterspout first offshore, a skyscraper of seawater that persisted for several minutes. No one knew what to make of the phenomenon. But even as it collapsed, a colossal Owl-Pig-Wallaby emerged from the depths and took flight over the city.

F2 was the only winged creature that we know of. It bore little resemblance to its American cousin, except in size, perhaps. By this time, joint science and military think tanks classed this sudden influx of kaiju as LSA (Large-scale Aggressors) but more common parlance dubbed them Fury-beasts. For the sake of speed and accuracy during the crises that spring, taxonomic debates were set aside and the monsters were just with an "F," followed by the number in the sequence they appeared in the world.

Another key feature of F2, in addition to its laser-breath, was its tendency to excrete vicious parasites from its skin. These were the first crab-dogs. They were unlike the ones we had aboard The Finasteride—instead of hose mouths, the mites of F2 had hooked beaks. Granted, many of them died once they detached from F2 because they didn't have enough membrane to sustain flight. If gravity did not kill them, the impact upon ground, roof, or mountaintop did its job. Some managed to live through their dive, though and anyone within scrambling distance would meet a terrible end, they basically stabbed people to death with their beaks and drank their blood and viscera until only deflated skin and hollowed bone remained.

Because it flew, the swath of calamity that F2 wrought was much larger. After Brisbane was razed to the ground, the beast visited similar fates upon New Zealand, New Guinea, and even Japan. I wished it had made it to Russia—now *there* was a nice big playground for it.

Unlike the others, F3 descended from space, and began dry-humping Istanbul during the small hours of May 7.

This LSA was wingless, so how could it be from space, right? The onlookers in the surrounding regions were intrigued by this phenomenon—F3 came down with a somersaulting motion, a clean, white-hot arc from the heavens that emanated a steady, disco-like beat.

The creature splashed cleanly into the Marmara, the shockwave shattering city walls that had stood for over a millennium. Byzantine scholars were outraged. The denizens of the city, even moreso.

It then unfurled into the shape of a starfish and began *rolling* rather than stomping over everything in its path. F3 three also differed from its predecessors in this way: it was only a torso, attached to over twenty dicks that equaled or exceeded the torso in mass, and each shot a thick stream of pink acid the consistency of cake frosting.

Istanbul doesn't have excessive sprawl by comparison with some other cities, so it became clouds of powder before the sun set that day. The people had a certain advantage, though: many fled through the ancient tunnels and then east along Anatolia. The monster did not follow them—for some reason it wouldn't leave the ruined city, even after it had rolled the same circuits non-stop for over a week. This had a strange effect: its dicks got bigger with every passing day, and its corrosive spray increased in range, eventually claiming Athens, Sevastopol, and even Damascus. The mega-starfish had a thing for very old cities. It wouldn't ever stop.

Theories emerged that F3 was the first gay kaiju.

This time, someone came up with a plan. Researchers had developed a bomb that used a hybrid sedative gas called [REDACTED] capable of bringing down even the colossal Fury-beasts. The modes of delivery had to be employed through trial-and-error, though. No one knew where the F3's main ingest points were. But it kept going around in the same circuit all over Istanbul, never varying. So, after repeated failures by tanks and warships, a joint coalition of airstrike and satellite, like the force that had shot off the arm of F1, ultimately gas bombed the creature into submission. Sweet dreams, dearie.

No one knew how long the chemical would be effective for, so a rather novel plan was put to work: since the LSAs were either impervious to weapons or healed from any wounds inflicted, they were prime candidates for surgical experimentation and research.

The powers that be gingerly shunted F3 into an industrial hangar in Eastern Europe that had apparently been custom-built for this purpose. The complex stretched for miles and couldn't be approached without at least ten levels of eye-pattern, thumbprint, and semen authentication. Anyone who tried to get close to the hangar was machine-gunned or burned to death. Many journalists and kaiju-rights activists retired early in this manner.

Now, I don't know exactly how Regalia Corporation became instrumental in what happened next. They hadn't been a huge conglomerate, and not a huge contender in the travel services industry at that time. Perhaps they had known the right contact person or even had an insider within the F3 slumber complex but I must give them props for both their sadism and their crudeness. The opportunity was there and they took it.

With science, surgical saws, and an astounding supply of technology on their side, Regalia transformed F3 into a luxury cruise ship by grafting a dura-steel framework into the body. The creature was surgically altered into a more conventional star-shape, so the grid wasn't especially difficult to imagine on an architectural basis. They also installed a rather ingenious central power source that had kept the creature asleep, yet pliable with electromagnetic commands into its brain and nervous system. The Lindsay, named in tribute to The Middle Piece from "The Human Centipede", also served as a huge broadcast antenna for satellite uplink should such a thing be required. In the unlikely scenario that F3 woke up from its trance chemically-induced by [REDACTED], the satellite could be used as a backup in case of emergency. It's funny when you see how strangely things are connected by the fucks in power. Thank cis patriarchy, right?

F3's lack of vertebrae and evenness of bone posed some complications, however. Despite the success of their initial experiments, nutritional plans, and macro-technology, the monster exploded before they could roll it out of the complex. Everyone within the blast radius perished, of course, and a kilometer-deep crater now marks the area. Geography professors say you could fit New York City inside of it. I think they should try that.

The careers of both F1 and F2 came to an even stranger end.

No one of us knows exactly how or why, but both Fury-beasts awoke for their dormancy and began battling each other over the Pacific Ocean. They'd visited upon opposite extremes of those waters, so it may have a territory thing, or they'd been incited by the death of their cousin. See, we'd been sure the creatures were indestructible, but that hadn't been the case with F3, although that might have been a suicide. Regalia Corporation learned a very hard lesson—never let the beast wake up from the effects of [REDACTED]. If it does, run away, far away.

F1 and F2 fought each using what unique powers their beings could afford them. F1 didn't have wings, but it used its regenerative powers to grow to such a height, it could stand in some parts of the vast water. The effect on the skies was catastrophic, causing freak weather and magnetic-storms. The Destructor Weapon fired at the beast from space as often as it could, but it just kept regenerating and growing vaster still. F2 also grew, but more horizontally. The three heads fought as one, using their heat rays to singe and flay their opponent. The wings also didn't help the atmosphere. Desperately, F2 kept trying to use its parasites to overwhelm F1, but it had little effect.

A joint military coalition tried to use the same [REDACTED] that had brought F3 down. It just made the beasts angrier. Finally, during one desperate, seething wrestle, F1 and F2 finally decided their playground was too small, and they both spiraled up past the atmosphere of the world and fled into the cosmos, a larger playing field.

Unfortunately, this is also how my parents disappeared. They were on a packed flight from Sakhalin, far from the region when during a rerouting the aircraft tried to avoid one of the storms wrought by the Fury-combat. The flight vanished somewhere above Polynesia. The wreckage was never found.

I'd been living in Brooklyn on about six cents and broken hopes. Things just weren't working out there. Sure, I'd been trying along with everyone else but I was really having trouble making ends meet, and the only way I could move back to Connecticut was to either tell my parents what was up, or detransition entirely. I'd worked too hard to let that happen. I'm sure everyone also thought so before they'd gone home, but I was going to find a way to keep myself there.

I'm glad I didn't.

F4 emerged from the ocean and destroyed New York on September 10, five days after I joined Roz in North Carolina.

But that time, Regalia Corporation was ready to up their game.

/05/

"I got his text," Sig said. "He's in the rest stop after exit 37."

The rain was less hardcore closer to Raleigh, but I still had the wipers cranked. I didn't know why I was letting this happen. I blamed myself for everything that had failed in New York, and now I was letting it happen down there, as well.

Something had to change.

Be careful what you wish for.

I saw the The Four Fucks van as we pulled into the rest stop. Jamison had parked it beneath a lone streetlight at the center of the lot. I pulled up next to it. Sig went to go in and look and came back a minute later.

"He's passed out in the back," he said. "And I think he pissed himself."

"I expected as much," I told him.

I got out of the car to stretch my legs and crack my elbows. I'd been up since seven in the morning and here it was like, almost two. I told Sig to hurry up and fuel the van so I could get home. Andrew got out of the car to wake his stupid drummer.

My hair kept blowing in my face from the wind. I didn't want to get into anymore discussions with them, I just wanted to find coffee somewhere. I was thinking of just sleeping there, and letting the three of them go back. But that didn't seem safe, maybe I could just call Roz, who lived just inside the city nearby.

I had to piss first, though. Jamison had managed to do at least that for himself. So there was something else I'd been denying myself, but unlike Jamison, I didn't want to be a child about it.

I see didn't see anything around, no tourist information, nothing. Some city welcome. The whole place looked unfamiliar, nightmarish, even, road signs riddled with buckshot and other cars going by at 120 MPH blasting chintz-ass CW stations and gospel talk. I'd pissed outside a few times post-transition, usually at Four Fucks house shows when the line to the bathroom was too long and I was feeling scared.

This place was pretty scary for different reasons, mainly because I was so far from New York, and I still wanted to go back. I'd still break out in hives whenever I was away from glass, concrete, flesh.

Sig was leaning against the van grille, smoking the Marlboros I'd bought.

"Do you guys have a flashlight?"

"I can look."

"Please hurry," I told him, then leaned in a little. "I need to squat."

He smiled a little.

"You didn't go back at the station?"

"You didn't *notice*?"

He looked around, shrugged, went in to open the glove box, took out a cheap black dildo, and flicked the switch.

Nothing.

I told him fuckit, just to stay there.

"I should go with you," he said.

"I'll be fine, just get your precious little dream boys ready to leave."

I went for the tree line. There was less lighting there but I didn't want anyone to see me. I hadn't pissed standing up in years, I had my pride. I didn't want poison ivy or some shit but I just wanted to get everything done with.

But it was only just starting.

The wind picked up again and I thought more of New York. I'd tried so hard. I'd need to apply those lessons if I was going to make it through with Sig, who had his own dreams of being a noise rock god. But sometimes it felt like I was only sticking around to help Roz with the insurance nightmare. We were both orphans. That fucks with you when it happens so suddenly and with no reconciliation. There was so much I'd wanted to say to mom and dad.

The woods felt soothing, the wind and foliage set a little isolation chamber for me so I used my cell phone to try and find a log or tree stump. I also didn't want to trip on anything. That would be just like me.

I angled myself so the piss would flow away from my feet. I had plenty to get rid of. I felt tainted, like there was more in life I had to be rid of. But it was the middle of an already fucked night and I didn't want to slide down that hole.

I spaced into watching the van and didn't notice the car pulling in right away. Its lights were off but it looked familiar. My piss was still coming and I tried to hurry it up.

The car stopped at a jagged angle, several feet away. I was like *oh great. Now this.*

Suddenly there was a pull at me, something deep within that made me rage my jeans back on and hit the ground, right into my own piss.

The wind stopped.

I peered over the log and watched two dudes carrying a body by the shoulders and feet. They were having trouble with it. They were coming straight at my hiding place.

"There," one of them said.

"Shit, no," his partner whispered. "Look." He nodded at the van. I had no idea how they hadn't seen it when they pulled in, it was right at the edge.

"There's probably no one in it."

"Its lights are off."

"We can just dump him," the guy holding the feet said. "We have to bring the 'jack over to—"

"Shut the fuck up," the other one said. "I know."

They were getting close.

Then my cell phone rang. I snatched at it to mute but they heard me. Fuckin' Sig. I stretched flatter so I couldn't see them. If I got up and ran for the van, maybe I could get past them. They'd maybe just drop the thing they were carrying and get me or maybe just shoot me in the back. I wanted to live.

"This isn't the place," one of them said. "Someone's here."

"Screw it. Put him in the trunk."

I heard them scramble back, thud the doors shut, and pull away again. I darted up just in time to see the receding Lexus, and the vanity plate I remembered from the gas station: "JAM ROD."

/06/

I didn't say anything to Sig during the trip back down. I didn't even ask him if he noticed the Lexus at all. Thankfully most of my piss had only gotten on my sleeve so I didn't have to ruin my car seat. The rain was letting up but the wind still blew at the car and I hand to grip the steering wheel hard as ever. My tension had ramped up with every mile we got closer to Wilmington.

I didn't want to get involved. Fuck the police. I had for-shit experiences with them in New York and of course North Carolina wouldn't be an improvement.

"Look, Carol," Sig said finally. "I'll try to make this up to you."

I felt thankful for the deflection.

"Don't even bother," I said. "I just think it's really telling that you don't stand up for me when they talk shit about me, even to other people at your shows, and then suddenly you need me to bail you out of a dumb situation like it's something I owe you?"

He didn't answer right away. He'd shown me so

much when I'd met him in New York. Now there was just a shell of what we'd been, and honestly I didn't feel like I could trust him with what I'd seen. And it still felt like my fault.

We rode in silence. At least we were getting "home." I was hoping Andrew wasn't too drunk himself by then to drive the van back. More for the sake of others on the road. Who knows what Jamison had accomplished before he ran out of gas.

I felt the distance between myself and Sig widening. Sure, he'd been one of the main reasons I had to leave New York but so something had changed in me, and I couldn't figure out what that was. Maybe after the destruction of New York by F4, it was like part of my dreams had been snatched away, but replaced with something else that was hiding from me. It felt really confusing and frustrating. So many of us think we'll never find "the one," but now that I had someone who wanted me, I didn't feel the same anymore. I felt like an asshole for that, ungrateful for the things I had.

I also felt regret over my sister, I wasn't there for her, while she had been the one to bail me out every time I'd fallen into trouble.

We were about to take the off-ramp when a car raced past us at high speed. It almost swerved into it because the road was so slick. My heart raced and I swore, watched the "JAM ROD" plate continue down the highway.

"What the fuck?" Sig broke from his trance.

"I don't know," I said. "Maybe he needs to get home and watch television."

The city looked dull on the horizon. I wondered

if F5 would come and make short work of it. I didn't know what made the creatures choose their cities. But it sure made life interesting every time.

We pulled into Sig's neighborhood. There were fire trucks and emergency vehicles up and down the blocks. Many trees had fallen and there was debris strewn all over the street, a tumbled pile of splintered households and dented lives.

We got out of the car because we couldn't go any further.

"Holy shit!"

The Four Fucks house was gone, along with the rest of the street.

/07/

Teemer was finally finishing up with me on the stand. It had been over an hour of him pretty much repeating the same question in different way, trying to catch something inconsistent in my account of the night.

The wreckage of their neighborhood didn't come from a Fury-beast. A tornado had touched down outside Wilmington and cut through their neighborhood. The weather didn't discriminate, and perhaps my diversion that night might have seemed like a mixed blessing, but that's not the way things turned out.

Teemer finally asked me, "So how sure are you that John Wilkes Booth and William Palmer are the two men you saw that night with the victim?"

"I told you, I saw them all *twice*. First at the gas station, and then at the rest stop."

"And how do you know the thing they were carrying out of the Lexus was a person?"

"Well, let's see," I glowered at the fuck. "Maybe the head, the *feet*? The bushy eyebrows?"

"There was enough to see his *eyebrows*?"

"Well if it wasn't Fuller," I asked, "what were they doing driving his Lexus?"

"Stealing a car isn't murder."

The courtroom gallery seemed stoic about this. I thought the whole thing was so damn obvious, but people can be stupid. I'd overestimated the value of coming forward as a witness. Regret wasn't a strong enough word by then.

"No, but carjacking can include exactly that," I said. "Maybe that never occurred to you."

"I have no further questions."

Teemer went back to the defense table. Booth and Palmer, definitely the pricks I'd seen that night, had gotten busted out of their own stupidity of using the victim's cell phone. They never stopped looking at me with a mixture of fascination and revulsion.

I often stared right back. I wasn't afraid of them. But there was something else.

The loss of my parents helped me make my decision to come forward as a witness. As I've said, these two idiots fucked themselves that night by using the cell phone and the GPS in the car. They'd driven south to get rid of the body and the victim had been heading north, to Raleigh.

I didn't know however, that Roderick J. Fuller, their victim was the father of Rod "Jam Rod" Fuller, a famous pro-wrestler with top billing in the WWF. In normal life, my report of the crime wouldn't have involved anything but my telling the truth to the pigs. But pigs being pigs, I got nothing but harassment from their end and from The Ratite Cult.

This is what happens when worlds collide.

The Ratites were a dark-web network of fascist keyboard commandos who made it their business to harass and ruin anyone they chose, often on a whim. The media hadn't been kind to me during the trial. Even though I was trying to do right by the bringing the perps to justice, my efforts only provoked a bunch of bullshit. They kept referring to me in the coverage as "Tranny Tale" and "Mister Wrestle-bitch."

The fandom of wrestling is apparently very protective of their little world. And when I ended up getting more coverage during the trial than Fuller, Booth, or Palmer, The Ratites picked up on that and began their campaign against me. I didn't ask for that shit, but it didn't matter.

The death threats first came over Facebook messenger and email. At first I was like—sure, I've never had my threatened before, ride that rocket, baby.

But then things got really serious. I had this librarian friend of mine tell me just how dangerous the cult was. They made Reddit seem like fun-time. They'd driven a few trans women to suicide, and had used whatever means in their power to harass people online, through the mail, and over the phone. The night a bullet came through my kitchen window, I figured it was time to leave North Carolina behind.

I called Roz and told her I might move back up north. She suggested The Ratites would follow me no matter where I went, that I should just try and ride it out until they grew tired and targeted someone else.

"I don't think I'm going to live long enough for that," I said.

Sig had been staying with his aunt. I'd let him go his own way. The Ratite harassment had turned into its own Fury-beast, stomping my life into so much powder. I didn't even have my bartending job anymore. Things had gotten fucked.

And all because I thought I'd done the right thing.

Roz asked me if I'd be open to going on a little trip with her, something to get away, rethink, refresh.

I told her I didn't think my life needed a vacation right then.

"It wouldn't be a vacation," she said. "It'll be a work-trip."

PART THREE

/01/

I opened my eyes to the worst pig-light ever. It felt like the bullshit the cops used to shine in at my nights back home, when I was trying to get it on with older retail guys in the backs of their cars. I hadn't figured a lot of things out about myself those days, but I still didn't appreciate the interruptions.

I sat up. A white, perfect beach bled into view. Had I won a vacation I hadn't been aware of? Sometimes I'd had dreams of being on vacation in some remote tropical place where nobody knew me from the news stories and I could just drink, smoke weed, binge 80s power metal, and get laid. This didn't look like that sort of place, though.

The beach stretched far, but I didn't see anyone else around. This made me suspicious of myself and my surroundings, which when you're trans happens at inopportune times and you just try to find a way home. The way home doesn't matter, so long as you get there.

I was just thinking that I'd missed the boat, yet again.

The sun was loud and getting on my nerves, so I got up and tried to find shade somewhere. A thick line of palm trees and brush foliage waved at me further up the shore, but there was a small beach hut only few yards away. I looked down at myself. I was stark naked. Instinctively my hands flew down to cover my bullshit, even though the place was isolated and no one would see me. None of that mattered, in that place, I didn't want to see myself like that, it was too bright and honest. Despite the warmth, everything felt uncomfortable and scratchy in my throat.

After a closer survey of the tree line, I saw a hut where I could hide from the sun and anyone else.

The sand was too hot so every step I took was a fresh burn at my feet. The longer I stayed out there, the more it hurt I just ended up running for the hut. There was a hippie-bead curtain at the entrance so I just snatched at it and dove in.

"FUCK!"

I tripped over something and almost landed right into the fire going at the center of the place. I rolled aside and shielded my body, thinking it was already too late, that I'd only escaped one burning to just fucked up by another, closer one. I hadn't expected any of this.

My eyes adjusted slowly to the interior of the hut. The small hole at the top of the roof let most of the smoke out. There was an auburn glare all around that felt soothing, made me think of the community I'd wished to find back in New York, a place of shelter, of safety. Had I finally found a place that would take me in? That always seemed too good to be true. I looked around. The place was unadorned, just some scratches that marked the walls at random diagonal intervals.

I knew then I wasn't alone.

My eyes took more of the place in, and sat up to face a grandad-looking Rastafakian. White dudes shouldn't wear dreadlocks.

"At last," he said. "You've finally decided to take back what's yours, Carol."

/02/

I opened my eyes to something different.

Laura was shaking me by the shoulder.

"We knew you could beat them," she smiled.

"What the fuck—"

I was covered in green cum from head to foot.

"Yeah, you literally got slimed," Jaden laughed. "I'll bet you only thought that happened in the movies."

I looked around. The place looked like one of those old spaceship control room Ed Wood movie sets, right down to its flickering diodes and rusty panels. The place also looked like it hadn't been swept in decades. What the hell for, anyway? The Leonardo wasn't important enough to be kept clean inside, even though it was the main energy source for the ship.

Laura explained that to me as I faced off with the black slime-beast and the strange force that trailed behind it, the control room door opened. Maybe it had a motion sensor. Jaden had pulled Roz inside, but Laura stayed back to come help me. But she didn't end up needing to.

"It swallowed you," she said. "I was going to try

and get you out but after it engulfed you, it glowed with some weird purple light, then it yacked you back up and fled back down the stairs. It left in a big hurry."

She wiped at my face with her sleeve. Gobs of the slime thudded onto the floor. I tried to get my bearings. There was the main console for The Leonardo, our only chance of sending a distress signal. Above this, the huge observation window gave us a nice panorama of the front of the ship. We were high up, and one look at the milieu that enveloped made it obvious that no one would be coming to help us.

The Sway had merged water and sky, up and down into a purple-pink vortex teeming with pterodactyls, tentacled Federal agents, crimson cyclopean caecodemon blobs that spat fireballs at each other as some sort of mating ritual, and all manner of saurian and cryptidae that I didn't have the patience to analyze by then.

Beyond the metal exo-skeleton of The Finasteride, our host-beast writhed in its usual troubled dreams but didn't seem awake yet. I had never appreciated the sheer enormity of the Fury-beast until I saw it from that far above. I'd also never fully appreciated how beautiful its skin looked—a paisley-pattern mottling of purples, grays, and greens that floated along the skin of the monster like bubbles in a lava lamp. Maybe seeing it all in a place where sunlight didn't exist anymore helped me see things for what they truly were all along.

"No wonder Brock wanted this," I muttered. "We're fucked."

"Nope," Laura said at my shoulder. "You still need to turn it up to full power."

"What, The Leonardo? What the hell for? There's no way back, remember? No one is coming to help us."

"We're not going back, we're going *through*, remember?"

I remembered just then, and something else.

"Where's Roz?"

Jaden led me to her.

My sister had huddled slightly upright in a corner, partially covered in coats and old blankets someone had found in the complex. She was pale, drained, trembling. I asked her what she needed. Her eyes opened a little, looked me up and down a moment, then she shook her head and went back inside her place.

I went back to Laura, who was studying the main console. I was hoping she knew it as well as Chloe claimed to have. Shit, I can barely set up a breakfast bagel, what chance did I have with that equipment?

"Brock must have infected her," I said. "You saw what he was doing to her up there."

Laura spoke into my ear.

"You should take the ship back."

"Why don't you, if you're so fuckin' smart?"

That came out a lot harsher than I had meant it to be. But Laura didn't blink.

"Look, so we're still going through," she went on. "Brock is doing this because The Sway is the only way to reach Kolkhorst."

"You never explained this to me, it makes no sense."

"Remember? Kolkhurst's located at the only point in the Pacific Ocean that is the direct opposite point of the planet as the center of The Hex Waters. That's why Brock steered us into The Sway. The island can't be approached from the water, nor from the air. But it can be approached from *underneath*. It's connected to The Hex Waters and the Caribbean by a straight line running through the center of the Earth. The Sway is the tunnel that gets us through that straight line."

"Well, that makes so much more sense now," I told her. "Thanks, anyway."

"Look, Carol, fuck you back, okay? If you don't want to hear about what's really going on, then don't ask me."

"How far do we have to travel through The Sway?"

"20,000 kilometers."

"When do retirement benefits kick in?"

"I don't know if you understand, Carol. The Sway pinches that travel distance to just a fraction of the time it would take anyone else above in the 'real' world."

"Oh."

"We're getting to Kolkhorst sooner than you think," Laura went on. "But the time we have left is running out fast. That's why you need to get The Leonardo back up and running, and take the ship from Brock. He doesn't give a shit about the end justifying the means. So, come on, just wake the fuck up, bitch."

"What?"

"Brock wants you for something. You have something only you can give. That's why he held your sister up in front of you like that."

"We just need to get the fuck out of here."

"The only way to it is *through* it," she said. "And that's also why it must be you, Carol."

"I don't want anything from Brock."

"Well, do you want him to get the better of you?"

I was so frustrated with how I'd let the winds of life blow me about in whichever direction. It wasn't right, to have so little control over my life. The one time I'd tried to do the right thing, I got screwed over. Doing the right thing again, to help these others find their way to some, any kind of safety, didn't seem like such a high calling by then.

But I did want to get my sister out of there. I owed her. Thing is, I also wanted to help Laura, and even Jaden her little snot-brother.

I needed to trust her. Chloe was gone, and I sure as shit didn't trust my own judgement at that time.

"Okay, then what?"

"You need to turn this antenna back on," Laura said. "It'll bring us back to full power. Also, it'll prod Brock out of hiding."

"F4 could wake up if we do that."

"Maybe that's what we need."

I looked out at the chaos and the beast and tried to accept it all as a new normal. Humanity has survived through adaptability, right? But then I wondered if the weirdest part of the journey was yet to come.

This was more in Laura's knowledge base than my own, so I told her about what I'd seen in my dream, the old guy in the beach hut.

"That's definitely him," she said. "That's Kutada. He's the sorcerer of the island. Brock wants something from him, but he's going to try and give it to you first."

"What's this?"

"It's something to do with taking control of The Sway, having it work for you or something."

"I don't even know where to start."

"Carol," Laura said to me, looking at me with scrunched eyebrows, "I've been all over the world. Believe it or not, so has Jaden. I can light your path. I know it's uncomfortable, but we need to use what we've got to get out of this. That's what makes us human."

I looked down at my crotch.

"So how do we turn this fucker on, then?"

Chloe had mentioned there was some sort of flesh key, but I didn't know what was involved. Laura brightened and immediately slid a tray out from the middle of the console. I was a simple raised metal slot, like something you grill sausages on.

"This is the flesh key, of course!" she said. "It has to be you, Carol."

"What?"

"The slime creature out there on the stairs fed off your bad memories," she went on, "but it also gave you something. You're the only one who can do this now."

"Can you start making sense, please?"

She pointed to the metal slot.

"You have to turn it on with your dick."

I'd forgotten about the discomfort, the dysphoria entirely. My thing had totally piped down after the encounter with the slime beast.

I pointed to my groin.

"I don't see how this is going to work," I said. "My hard-on went away."

"I'll help, then."

Laura grabbed me by the collar and kissed me deep. All too briefly, I forgot where the hell I was, and how I'd gotten there. A wave crashed through my nerve endings and I felt both of our pricks inflate at the same time, and that time I *wanted* it. She pressed up against me and that made my desire for her scream for fuck, no matter where we were. We were both taking charge of something we both needed, and finally I thought things might be okay. I wanted it to last.

She broke loose, licked the tip of my nose, and wheeled me around towards the console.

"Now, turn on this bullshit," she said.

I didn't even ask the others to turn around. I inched myself down, grabbed hold of my *flesh-key*, and flopped the stupid creature onto the cold dura-steel power slot of The Leonardo.

/03/

A squeal of digital interference rose from the panels and all the lights came on full blast. The entire complex shook with anger. Outside, The Sway began to invert and buckle from within.

"Is this normal?" I asked Laura.

"Define *normal*."

I took my meat off the slab and re-tucked it. The swelling hadn't gone down yet, so it was like trying to hold a watermelon with my asscrack. The dysphoria had alleviated somewhat, though, which was a welcome change.

"Look!"

One of the side panels slid out from the wall and revealed a standing arsenal. The entire world of hope opened up as the layers unfurled: I counted fifteen power-cell electro-meg AG44 pulse laser rifles, each with a pulse grenade launcher, eight old-school, tried-and-true shotguns, and a full-800 range of ace-ten gauge sniper rifles.

We were no longer helpless.

Brock then appeared on the huge panoramic screen above the console.

"Thank you, Carol," he sneered. "Very well done,

we couldn't have planned this better."

The captain's mutations had taken an even more spectacular turn. Where there had once been tendrils, tentacles, and other auxiliary appendages, there were now pinwheels, self-contained suns, and the faces of pleasantly surprised babies. Brock had also liquefied and ballooned into a sort of cloud-like formation, expanding and contracting his form into all manner of concepts. He just couldn't make up his mind of what he wanted to be, so he kept replacing one state of being with another.

"Now we can begin the final stage of our journey," he went on. "Now that The Finasteride is running at full power, we can ride with The Sway instead of against it, and push through to the island."

"If you're talking about Kutada," Laura chimed in, "I think you're going to find he doesn't want to help your power grab."

"Oh, we're going to have a fair exchange with the old sorcerer, trust me."

I looked over a Laura, then back out at the sleeping titan.

He was going to return F4 to its owner.

Brock floated aside to let us better appreciate the mutations still taking place in Quintal, his security forces, the casino patrons, and the rest of the crew. Each had their own unique take on monstrosity and depravity. The mutated passengers formed a ring around them and pulsed and buzzed with gorged mosquito bliss. Brock was remaking the world in his own image.

And we were next.

"You're fucked up," I told Brock.
He shrugged.
"And yet I'll be the one to survive this."

/04/

Laura was navigating the controls by trial and error. She was saying something about regulating the proper dosage of [REDACTED] to keep F4 from regaining full consciousness. But she also said that the supply was dwindling, and that the beast would awaken soon and probably not be in the best mood when it found a huge metal cage grafted into its body, including but not limited to the propeller shaft up its rectum.

I kept looking at Chloe on the screen. She didn't look like a willing conspirator. She was covered in the same snot as I had been, only this was more of a reddish color, with streaks of grey. She looked half-asleep. That asshole Quintal stood behind her, propping her up by the shoulders.

She opened her eyes.

"I'm sorry, Carol."

"That's enough," said Brock. "Look, people, you've obviously seen the antenna isn't going to help you at all. No one is coming to rescue you. We're almost through the vortex and once we get to the island I'm going full-power."

"Kutada isn't going to give up his pet," Laura told him. "F4 will just eat you when you try to wake it up."

"I have a way around that," he said. "But first, why don't you all just make this easy on yourselves and surrender? Come on back up to the deck. No use in postponing the inevitable. Then we can all be on the same crew and once F4 is fully within my control—"

I lunged for one of the AG44 pulse laser-rifles. It felt like a large robot dog in my arms. I hadn't fired one of those things since Sig had taken me target practicing in North Carolina, back when the harassment by The Ratities was in full frenzy.

I made sure he could see the weapon.

"We're not giving up, fuckface," I told him. "We are coming to get her."

"You can go," Roz muttered behind me. "I'm staying here."

I turned. She was standing up, perhaps to face the prickwad who'd made her so sick. Her skin was turning grey and boils had formed on her skin. Having seen Quintal and Brock's other subordinates on the security force, her changes were manifesting, as well. There was plenty to worry about, and my faux-machismo wasn't going to help her.

But I knew we had to stop Brock, somehow.

"I promise you'll be safe from the crab-dogs," The Captain said. "You won't have any trouble getting here."

"Does that have an off switch?" I asked Laura. "Or can we at least pot him down?"

"Don't bother. I've got just the thing to convince you."

The screen chimed and fizzled out.

"We're going to get out of here," I said. "If he wakes

the beast up, The Finasteride is going to be even more unstable. How much further is it to the island?"

"There's no way of knowing," said Laura. "None of the gauges will work and I can't even tell how much [REDACTED] is left for F4. It could wake up any second, really."

"Then you know what? We've got nothing to lose."

I turned to my sister and pointed to the rack of weapons.

"Pick one, even if it's one of the light ones," I said. "Because you're fuckin' coming with us."

I asked Jaden if he'd ever fired a gun. He said no, so I suggested he just pick up one of the sniper rifles to use as a club. Those crab-dogs were going to fuck with us, for sure. And I didn't know what was going to happen with the Barbapapa slime creatures, whether or not the pulse-rifles would have any effect. But I also remembered that the one I'd faced down before hadn't done much to harm me. I didn't know if its friends had an appetite for trans women, though. Maybe they were so secure in their slimehood that they'd admit to something like that to their friends and family.

We were just gearing up, shouldering and belting as many firearms as we could carry, when another convulsion rocked the ship. The dura-steel groaned. The console was flashing some code I couldn't make out.

"It's a proximity alert," Laura said to us.

Outside, The Sway was darkening, and less hectic.

Time, for what it was in that place, was running out.

The vents just below the ceiling began to ooze that familiar black goop in numerous, ropey streams.

"I think we get the hint," Laura said.

"Let's do this," I said. "I'm either going to get Chloe

or I'm going to shoot her in the face."

Roz gasped when the slime began to congeal and reconstitute once it reached the floor. The material wasn't forming one slime-beast, but many. Their huge mouths opened and breathed out an odor of old musty books combined with swamp rot. They looked hungry.

I thought I'd test my weapon, so I wheeled around and fired a laser bolt into the nearest sooty snot column. Laura had also picked up a pulse rifle and joined me in the volley. The monster's eyes bulged a moment, as if astonished by our friskiness, then its gaping toad mouth inverted into a smile. It then broke down into several hundred raindrops that dispersed evenly to its fellows at either side of it, each of whom grew exponentially in turn.

"I think it's time to leave," Jaden suggested.

I raced to Roz, who had taken my advice and adopted a sniper rifle to use as a blunt weapon, of sorts. It was better than nothing, but I knew I'd need to keep watch for her because she was looking more and more sick, as Brock's corruption kept progressing inside of her. I took her by the elbow and yelled at Jaden to lead the way.

Our movement was hindered by the weight of the extra weapons we'd strapped onto ourselves. I'd been thinking ahead but speed was going to have to be a more important factor than how much firepower we had. We could always find more, but then how could I be sure? We'd not gone through basic training—we'd been up all night fighting a nightmare we couldn't wake up from.

"Out the door!" I called to everyone. "Back the way

we came!"

Jaden slammed the control room door behind us. I knew that wouldn't hold the slime creatures for long, and I was right. Again, the creatures liquefied afresh and seeped in a puddle beneath the door. It was still hungry for—well, if not for me, then the others I cared about, even Jaden. His being Laura's younger brother was not of undue influence, but we also needed him in case we needed to find a secret way.

Our descent down the stairwell was easier, of course, even though the ship was listing to starboard again.

"No one look back!" I shouted to everyone as I took up the rear. "Don't look back! Just keep moving!"

"She's right!" from Laura. "Momentum will get us through!"

Brock was going to deal with us however he wanted to once we were exposed to the unnatural elements on deck of The Finasteride, so there was only so much we could control. We had some pretty badass weapons, finally. I was not in a mood to be fucked about anymore.

I was going to break Chloe out.

Jaden reached the bottom foyer and we pulled back together. Laura read my mind and together we fired a fresh volley at the approaching wall of slime. It dispersed once again, but the splat flew at us. Shit!

We got out and slammed the door just in time. I heard the impact and knew the creature was just going to recollect itself and come for us again.

We were greeted by a semicircle of Quintal's security forces, some fifty of the still-mutating cis bros, their skin greening, bubbling, their limbs and trigger fingers becoming more ophidian. Our weapons all came ready.

Quintal was the first to speak, his voice moose-like, "Welcome back, fags! Glad you decided to rejoin the party!"

"Like fuck we are!" Laura answered him, her rifle pointed at Quintal's undulating face.

"Yeah," I said. "Get the fuck out of our way or you'll be the hors d'oeuvres"

The Sway roiled around The Finasteride, still. But the vortex less turbulent. I figured this meant we were almost through the center of the planet and coming out the other side, to Kolkhorst Atoll, and its sorcerer.

"You know, *Mister* Carol," Quintal sneered at me, "We've watched you for a long time, ever since the trial. You thought you suddenly were going to make a name for yourself, but there's no one like Jam Rod Fuller in all of pro-wrestling. No one steals his spotlight. I'm glad we were instrumental in stopping you."

"Fuck," from Laura.

"That's right," he went on, slithering up to us. "You were our most successful campaign. You were exactly what The Ratities needed to get our message across, that we would pinpoint and knock down as many fag-left SJW's as we could. We noticed a real tipping of the scales once we were done with you."

"You're from The Grotto," I said. "Your leadership isn't scattered. You're all in one place."

I didn't know Quintal had been involved in the cult, but I knew of The Grotto and that appealing to this fuck's sense of vanity and ego might tease some information out of him. I'd promised myself that if I ever found out where the headquarters of The Ratites was located, I'd crush the place beneath my high-heeled boots. They'd made me lose my job, my home, my boyfriend. Worse, they'd made me lose *time*—and that pissed me off more than anything. I'd had no interest in upstaging Jam Rod. He'd put out a plea for any witnesses to his father's murder to come forward. All I could think of was the loss of my own parents, and how their unknown fate was weighing down on both me and my sister. I should have reported what I'd seen that night at the rest stop anonymously, but pigs, right? I was stupid to think I could do the right thing.

"The Grotto isn't your concern." Quintal said, then the asshole addressed me by my deadname. "You just need to come with us. We'll be arriving at our destination in a few minutes, and once we've come out of The Sway, you're going to want to have walls around you."

"He's right about that," Laura whispered to me.

Roz was still holding up her rifle in front of her like a baseball bat, perhaps recalling what Brock had done to her.

I didn't see the crab-dogs anywhere, but I knew the slime-creature would be up with us at any moment.

Again, I glanced back. Sure enough, the dark ooze seeped from beneath the main doors of The Leonardo. The puddle had legs.

We were trapped.

"Let's just ice these fuckers," I told our group. Roz and Jaden didn't have much firepower but Laura and I could at least take a few of the bastards with us.

"Well?" Quintal jeered, wild-eyed "We're waiting…"

We raised our pulse rifles, I aimed for the bullseye of Quintal's shit face. But before we could fire, the slime creatures slithered around us and made straight for the security force. They saw the goop closing in on them and even Quintal stepped back a few paces.

Just then, the sky exploded in a roaring sweep of laser fire. The purple-green tube of cirrus clouds parted to reveal the newest arrival. The trio of Owl-Pig-Wallaby faces was unmistakable. F2 had returned from wherever.

I'd never seen the entity in flesh and feather, except in news stories. The only winged Fury-beast known to our world, its epic scale made quite the entrance. None of us knew why it had come, though. My main fear was that it had tired of fighting F1 up in the cosmos, and wanted a new sparring partner in F4. If anything could wake the host of The Finasteride out of its [REDACTED] stupor, it was another Fury-beast.

The force of the breach blew us back against the dura-steel as we watched the slime-creatures re-gather into a continuous wave that hovered over Quintal and his goons a moment, then after savoring their collective disbelief a moment, crashed down onto them all. The outline of the warriors melted down as swiftly and steadily as when water washes away salt.

Still, I didn't trust to hope. Considering the changes Brock has inspired in his underlings, I just figured Quintal and his shitheads would just become more powerful with the help of the slime creatures. But then the distant, familiar screech of the crab-dogs reached our ears and we steeled ourselves for a fresh onslaught.

But F2 got to us first.

And yet there was something different about the

monster as it hovered above the main deck. There was a metal box dangling from its prick. The box sprouted bullhorns and addressed us.

"Come with me if you want to live."

Whoever this pilot was, he'd taken some hints from Regalia Corporation and had managed to graft a steering/control device onto the modest anatomy of the Fury-beast and used it to full advantage.

As the box descended to deck-level, the slime-creatures formed a perimeter around us. At the base of this wall, a barrage of crab-dogs was trying to muscle through and get at us, but failing miserably. It was difficult to stand up straight as the winds generated from F2's wings blew us back still further against the front doors of The Leonardo. Then, like the best savior moments of any space opera trope, a ramp extended from beneath the chassis.

I recognized the sorcerer from my dream. Kutada looked shorter and younger than he'd first appeared to me. I could tell he also had a mad hard-on.

The crab-dogs kept wailing and screaming, and as a few of them took a running start and finally managed to leap over the wall of slime, we took our cue and raced into the madman's welcoming arms.

Laura got a few shots in for good measure, but that only encouraged a fresh barrage of the little pests. Roz was definitely flagging, so I shoved her up the ramp and Jaden led his sister in. As I went in last, Brock's voice filled The Sway:

You're only postponing the inevitable, Carol.

Suck my dick! I called back, and once the ramp doors slammed shut behind us, we took the fuck off.

/04.1/

The atoll looked like a perfect circle as we approached from below. I'd never once considered how the geological formation of a place in the world can affect the human mind, be they native or colonizer. But this felt like we were flying to the moon. I wondered if we would be able to breathe there, and what the sorcerer had planned for us.

Of course, Brock had floored The Finasteride engines and was hot on our heels. But Kutada assured us that F2 could outrun any other Fury-beast—it had the advantage of true flight, and velocity lent us speed, along with determination.

I knew I was leaving Chloe behind, and I felt like a failure, yet again. Laura tried to assure me we would get her away, but she failed to encourage me. Roz, of course, told me the bitch wasn't worth a squirt of piss, that she'd never have done the same for me if our places were switched.

Kutada steered the creature with a strong and steady hand. I'd never once wondered what the wizard looked like—he only stood about four and a half feet tall, looked to be about mid-40s, and dressed like a retail clerk at Best

Buy. I wouldn't have taken him for a necromancer, but that's why they're good at what they do. Staying low-key can be survival, and don't I know it.

He told us we were approaching the lagoon. We were almost through The Sway. The rush of air behind our winged host-beast roared with chaos.

And sure enough, we arrived at the mysterious island with all the subtlety of an old queen sashaying down Broadway with arm full of pizzas and trailing a peacock on a leash. The purple-green-grays of the vortex gave way to earthly blue tropical skies and billowing white summer clouds. The white sands of the atoll reminded me of my dream, so full of enigma and promise.

Kutada reined F2 and landed us smoothly onto what must have been his home part of the beach. I recognized the hut but there were certain other signs of cohabitation. The sorcerer powered down his electronics and spoke a single word to F2—*sanctuary*.

The Owl-Pig-Wallaby heads each grunted then purred with sleep. It was as if the guy had just flicked a switch. He had not needed [REDACTED] to lull the creature into slumber. He had the Fury-beast under his control—and why not? Most people knew that he had been the one to summon them to the world, anyway. I just wondered if he could perhaps do the same for F4, and work against Brock in some way. But I had a feeling that was up to me, and only me. I didn't want to accept that responsibility, no matter how powerful.

We shouldered our weapons and shuffled down the open ramp onto the hot sand. I wished we had sunglasses, the glare was obnoxious. My prick got hard again, and that was a distraction I didn't want.

Especially when we saw what decorated the beach.

Each human head was spaced evenly, about seven feet apart, all the way down the shoreline. They all faced the massive lagoon. The winds swept through their hair, sometimes make them look like gorgons with their eyes closed.

"Are they dead?" Roz asked him. "Do you have the same thing planned for us, psycho?"

Kutada shook his head.

"No, they are only asleep. They all dream of the great homecoming for my children. And only when they are all here can I awaken the beach heads from the spell."

"Those are people," Jaden objected. "It's not fair. What if they drown?"

"The tides don't reach them, trust me. They are all well cared for."

"I hope you give them all sunscreen," I muttered.

Kutada led us up to this larger bungalow that looked like it had been spliced together from old shipping crates, vines, and straw. True Pacific island living. I definitely wanted some shade. Even though this place was supposed to be part of this nether-zone, unapproachable except from beneath, the sun felt real enough, and oppressiveAF. Trans women are supposed to stay out of direct sunlight, with our hormones and shit.

It was dark inside the wizard's house, and right away I thought he was going to add our four heads to his collection. But instead he grunted, drew aside a palm leaf he'd been using as a window shade, and invited us to sit around his fire pit.

Laura couldn't resist her cryptozoologist urge and

asked Kutada why he'd summoned the Fury-beasts into an already troubled world.

"Our place in the universe is small," he began. "Humanity needed to be reminded of this. America especially has prided itself on its isolationism, when really there wasn't much to be proud of."

I could attest to that much. Where else would something The Ratite Cult, whose only M.O. was cyberbullying and terrorism, be able to thrive? In a nation with a small-dick complex that must overcompensate with bluster.

"That is why I sent two beasts to America," he went on. "Also remember, that alchemy is the original science. Medicine was sacred magic, once. It still is. And I summoned the LSAs to remind you all that certain things cannot just be explained away. You have to experience the unexplainable to believe in it."

"Yeah, like bullshit."

The sorcerer faced me, surprised that I wasn't having it. I kept after him.

"What makes you think you're so special?" I asked him. "Like you're the one to teach us something about ourselves by sending a bunch of monsters to attack our cities? Sure, I ended up having no love for New York but I was planning on going back once my life came together finally."

"What makes Captain Brock think he's so special?" he countered. "Knowledge is the magic we need, the true gateway to power. But you should put magic to good use. You can't seize power just for the sake of having it. You have to *want* to know what makes it special. This is where your captain comes up short."

"He's convinced that you can give him power."

"He dreams big."

"The Sway changed him into a monster," I said. "He's always had a mean streak but now he's more fucked up than ever."

"By the same token, what makes you think *you* are so special?"

"Well, gee whiz, where to start, maybe because I'm *trans*?"

"That goes for the two of us," Laura offered. "But I'm not that special."

"You've got a few degrees, Laura."

She shrugged, what was that to us by then? We were sitting on an island that didn't really exist. Were we in "Lost"?

Also, we'd been through The Sway—how did we know we were still really alive? No one goes through a time-space portal unchanged. But I couldn't really gauge in there was anything different about me. I felt badly that I hadn't protected Roz well enough. She was looking tired and sick.

"Consider this also, Miss Stratham," Kutada went on. "What made you decide you could help as a witness in the Fuller trial? What made you decide to transition? No, no need to answer. It's all very simple. We see a problem in the world, we decide to do something about it, rather than let ourselves get blown about like ash in a wind."

"Or a tornado," I smiled.

That was the storm that took Sig and The Four Fucks House down. F4—classed *violent* on the Fujita scale, the thing where they measure tornado severity.

F5 is the highest score.

Kutada hadn't finished his sermon.

"When something 'sucks', as you call it, it's up to us to change it. As sure as we all live and breathe, we all have *agency*."

"How much agency do those people buried outside on the beach have?"

He ignored my question.

"I've seen your past in my night-fires, Carol. You think your failures in New York, Wilmington, and on The Finasteride are things that *define* you. But you're here on this island for a purpose. You're bringing F4 back to its home."

"What? Brock's bringing F4 because he wants something from you."

"F4 was hoping to find you there in New York," he said. "It was drawn to you."

"You mean I can wake it up."

"You can wake it up."

"Won't it be pissed off, and decide to eat us?"

We heard a tremendous sonic boom outside, followed by a monstrous splash.

"Only if you let it."

/05/

They hadn't come through the lagoon. Brock had perhaps miscalculated his entry. But there it was.

The Finasteride was covered in black snot and writhing tentacles. Crab-dogs ran to and fro, pausing occasionally to lick each other's assholes. The mutants had increased in number, I figured they'd devoured the rest of the survivors. I didn't see Quintal, but his security forces amassed behind Brock. They were slithering down a ramp fashioned from the flexible goop of the creatures. They were coming straight for us.

I didn't see Chloe.

"Okay," I said, making sure my rifle was at full power. "Let's rock."

I kept the trigger depressed, and the gun unleashed a steady stream of dura-steel death.

Laura joined me in the barrage of laser fire and stood her ground.

"I guess we're doing this again," she said.

"Looks that way."

Even as our conjoined fire mowed down a steady stream of crab dogs and the twisted screaming flesh of former passengers, nothing seemed to even phase Brock who simply waded through the carnage, indifferently sliding through shattered carapaces and writhing, screeching bleeding flesh on his tentacles. Kutada had disappeared. I didn't know what good the sorcerer was going to be anyway—to me he was still just a bunch of talk. But Roz and Jaden were waving their arms at us, trying to get us to move into the tree line and fall back ass empty magazines clattered to the ground and our supply of ammunition dwindled. I told Laura we should leave the last stand for another time, when we either had more firepower or if we could get the upper hand over Brock somehow. Laura and I ran for it. She was a few paces ahead of me when a huge javelin whizzed by and caught Laura in the center of her back. She fell face down onto the sand. I screamed.

Brock had thrown the projectile.

The diminished enemy forces had gained on us, now made up predominantly of Quintal's goons and some surviving passengers, and crab dogs. That fucker's grin filled his face when he saw me. He then glanced down at Laura's injury and he sprayed green cream from his neck gills. He made a lewd gesture at us and laughed.

I was too numb with shock to even bother shooting at him.

Roz came out to help me pick Laura up and we dragged her by the shoulders into the trees as Brock's forces massed on the beach and started cheering.

Roz and I had Laura face down on the cold

dura-steel and together we pulled the spear from her. It collapsed at our feet like a huge pad thai noodle. Laura cried out. I held her. She was hemorrhaging and shivering. I didn't want her to go.

"I'm going to get these assholes," I promised her. "I'm going to fuck them up."

Jaden was weeping, he couldn't look at his sister like that, dying right in front of him.

I couldn't get enough of seeing her, even in that state.

She looked back into me.

"I'm cold, Carol," she said.

"I know, I'm sorry I got you into this mess."

"You didn't. I wanted to come with you."

I held her tighter and kissed the top of her head repeatedly, shushing as she whimpered. After she was gone, I stayed like that.

/06/

We were circling the atoll. F2's speed ramped down as it passed over its sibling, perhaps to not disturb it with its massive wings. I was surprised the beast could still be sleeping during that chaos. This was supposed to be the grand homecoming, after all. But very little made sense in that place.

Roz had covered Laura with a blanket. I stood and peered out at the beach. Brock's forces had congealed around Kutada's bungalow, while Brock screamed triumph and demanded Kutada come and reward him for returning F4. Occasionally, he got bored begging for the wizard to show up and asked me how my 'side bitch' was doing in a petulant whine conjoined with threats of what would happen to Chloe if I didn't bring the wizard to him.

Roz was looking a little better. I didn't know how much of Brock's poison remained in her, but she was fighting it off well.

Kutada appeared beside us out of nowhere.

"Thanks for standing with us, asshole," I answered

him. "Laura paid with her life."

"I know, I saw. I'm sorry."

"Yeah."

"I couldn't let Brock gain access to me. Not yet. The time is not right."

"I thought time was bullshit here, anyway."

I looked down at the black pike that had killed Laura. It was undulating like a maggot. We had a slime creature with us.

"Yes," Kutada said. "You know why it hasn't attacked? You have more control over this than you realize, Carol."

I remembered how the creatures had gone after Quintal security forces, right before F2 rescued us from the deck of The Finasteride.

"You just need to assert your control," he said. "But you need to *want* that."

Roz looked at me and shook her head, her eyes wide. *No.*

"Get up," I told the black slime.

It stopped writhing, coiled in on itself, and then stood on end.

Then the sky outside convulsed, and we felt a huge shockwave, as if the universe had just had a spontaneous orgasm.

"Holy shit," from Jaden.

Out the window we saw F1, the upright axolotl and the biggest of them all, land feet first into the ocean. It waved its massive arms and roared to announce the start of the party. There was plenty to celebrate, after all, a joyful reunion of the Fury-beasts with their master.

/07/

I could still save Chloe, I was reminded by Brock's continued invective hurled from the beach. If he wanted me, he was going to fucking *get* me.

The air felt thick and hot. I had my gun in my arms and Laura's slung across my back. I was going to make squid fricassee of Brock and his subordinates. This was no longer mutiny, this was justice.

As we crept deeper into the island towards a central lagoon, Roz cried out. I turned and saw the cause of her outburst. There, among the dozy heads, lay our parents, Michael and Eustice Stratham. No wonder there were so many heads around the atoll—their flight had 249 passengers and crew. They'd all ended up here. Whether or not this was enough proof for the insurance company back on the mainland, I didn't know. But they weren't dead, that was the thing. But they also weren't ready to wake up.

"That's right," said Kutada. "They are what drew you to this place, to me, to the beasts. And now we're all together."

"Yeah, fuck you back," I said. "One big happy family."

I pointed to the other heads, up and down the beach.

"They all have relatives, too, you know. Maybe they're wondering where they went. They never found the wreckage of the plane."

"They'll never find it. Not here. But you can take them all home after this."

"Then what makes me so special?"

"Didn't we have this conversation before?" Roz asked.

"Perhaps you should ask yourself that, Carol."

I looked at the waiting slime creature, its mouth puckering like a fish.

"I'm the witness," I said.

"Yes," Kutada nodded. "But everyone knew you'd be of more use here. The Fuller trial didn't need your help, but the beasts do. You can protect them from those who would invade the nest."

The sorcerer chinned toward the lagoon.

Brock was no longer content to simply wait and was crashing through the tropical tree line on the other side of the lagoon. Quintal and the others followed, their outer bodies undulating. My own slime creature quailed at the sight. But I finally knew what to do. I wanted it enough, so I would have it.

I concentrated all of my effort into a single thought, and then spoke the key word.

"*Sanctuary*," I said to the enemy. And then, "You can follow my banner, instead."

Some of the slime following Brock quivered uncertainly but there wasn't enough time to do much of anything because Brock threw himself at me, his ibex horns aimed at my chest and his tentacles seeking to grasp and crush me. I fired round after round at his lashing, grasping tentacles; yet, no matter how many I severed, more replaced them, like the mythical hydra. Having exhausted my ammunition, I gripped my trusty crowbar and charged, at him screaming with ultra-trans hate. Bludgeoning his head didn't seem to faze him very much, but he screamed like some hideous hybrid of a 56k dial-tone and a pig achieving climax when I gouged out his left eye and drove the point of it deep into his head. However, in spite of my angry lashing at his stupid petulant face, his tentacles encircled my waist. As he held me up, Quintal strode up behind him, leveled a shotgun to the back of Brock's head and unloaded the entire load. Brock's head exploded like a melon, all avarice and ambition culminating into that one sad mess.

"You never had any vision, Brock" he bragged over his captain. "You wanted to *rule* this world, and I want to change it—I have *the vision*—purge it all of the faggot SJW's and their fucking agenda, exterminating the normies and making anime real—"

Quintal's victory speech was cut short as a boney phallic spine shot from Brock's back into his midsection. Enraged, Brock turned on his traitorous subordinate and they began to roll across the ground Quintal pumping rounds into Brock's fleshy body as Brock impaled, clawed and squeezed him. As they rolled to the edge of the lagoon, one of Brock's tentacles touched it and immediately began withering. As he reared up in pain and shock dangling Quintal over the poisonous water; I took my chance charging Brock, and shoved him into the Lagoon as the two rolled screaming as their bodies scalded away into the depths.

Relieved as I was, Chloe was still aboard the F4 and in addition to setting her free, there was something else I had to help with.

I told everyone to wait on the beach and stepped onto the slime panel. Right away, the collective strength of the creatures bore me up toward the deck in a huge undulating motion. It was the fastest escalator I'd ever ridden.

As I approached the top, I saw the line of crab-dogs waiting for me, those toothed hoses chomping. All I had to do was whispered the word *sanctuary* aloud and they all dispersed, cowering. Then they all got bored and started fucking each other's buttholes, forming a single ball of beige cryptid lubricity that soon rolled off the deck and into the waters below.

I found Chloe in the control room of The Leonardo. She'd been cocooned in a hard shell of the dark slime. I broke it apart with a single exhalation and she slumped forward into my arms. I kissed her hard on the lips, being the smoking-hot trans dykes we still were, and her eyes twitched open.

"Holy shit," was the first thing she said, and then, "how did we get here?"

"I can't account for you," I said. "I figure Brock stashed you here to force my hand once he had me prisoner. Or force my dick, rather."

"Yeah, he tried that with me, also," she said, gesturing toward the key slot of the control panel. "Tried to get me to wake F4 up."

"Only this time it's for real. We can both do it."

She looked at me like I was high and asked me why the fuck we would do that. I told her I knew what I was doing and that we'd be safe. In fact, waking up the beast was the right thing to do. Then she brought up a good point—The Finasteride had been surgically grafted into the creature's indestructible anatomy, when it woke up to find itself, well thus encumbered, wouldn't it freak out? Or just blow itself up, as F3 had done?

I told her I knew what F4 wanted, and that I could provide it.

I helped her up and let her try to collect herself.

"What about The Sway?" she asked. "And Brock?"

"I know how to make The Sway work *for* us this time. And Brock's not—not here."

I stopped short of saying he'd drowned in the lagoon—I'd only seen him go under, and I didn't really know what he could withstand with his cephalopod-mutations. Perhaps he was enjoying the toxicity of the waters.

"Look, I know what I want now," I said to Chloe. "And I think I know what F4 wants. But I'm going to need your help."

She looked over at the key slot.

"Both of us?"

"Yeah, but once it's done, we're probably going to have to get the fuck out of here in a hurry."

Sanctuary.

We watched F4 from down on the beach. It was groggy, moving a little slow, but I don't know how long it had been kept asleep by all of the [REDACTED] they'd kept pumping into it through The Leonardo. Now that I was there, to rein The Fury-beasts and The Sway alike, it wouldn't need to sleep anymore. I felt like I could use some, though.

And that reminded me.

I walked further up the beach to where Roz was standing, trying to keep our mom and dad's heads shielded from the blaring sun. Kutada and Jaden stood by, looking around nervously at the other heads that stretched along the shore as far as the eye could see. I wondered how I was going to get them all awake, but then remembered I needed Kutada to do it. I'd done everything he'd tasked me with, hadn't I?

That's when Quintal crawled up out of the lagoon, gasping and choking. I went to him and he stopped short of my boots. His skin was peeling and dripping off him in sheets.

I pointed Laura's pulse rifle at him (I'd given the other one to Chloe, in exchange for sharing her dick with mine in The Leonardo control room).

"Please help me," Quintal wheezed. "The Captain tried to eat me in there."

"Oh, *you* can eat me, motherfucker."

"Carol, I'm sorry."

"Sorry shit," I scoffed. "You helped The Ratities long enough to know. Tell me where I can find them. Where's The Grotto?"

"We're just fucking around," Quintal whined. "It's free speech, it's in the First—"

"You made me fear for my fuckin' life," I said. "You made me lose my boyfriend. You drove *two* other fuckin' trans women to commit suicide. All because you didn't want all that SJW-shit shoved down your throats, right?"

I gently kicked his body over so he was supine, like a beetle stuck on its back.

Pathetic fuck.

I faced him.

"Open your mouth."

Quintal shook what was left of his pulsing head.

"Open your fuckin' mouth, you worthless wannabe Nazi fuck."

His lips parted, his green saliva gummy. I didn't want that shit on Laura's gun barrel but this was *Quintal* I had at my feet. I wanted the answers.

I stuck the gun in his mouth. His flesh was smoking in the sunlight, disintegrating from within

"Do you want this to be quick or slow?" I asked him. "Where's the Grotto?"

He shook his head again.

"I'm going to count to—"

His lips moved and he tried to say something. I took the gun out of his mouth.

"New York," he said. "Fishkill, New York."

At that, Quintal's head caved in beneath the coiling tentacles of Captain Brock, glistening with phosphorescent lagoon mucus. His flesh was sloughing off of his body and most of his tentacles were gone along with one of his horns, yet still he seemed dangerous. I fell back onto the sand and aimed the pulse rifle at him.

I pulled the trigger, but the rifle jammed.

"No matter what you try and prove," he snarled at me, "I'm getting what I came all this way for."

He gathered his mass for a fatal strike, but he

twitched as Chloe unloaded the magazine of her Sig Sauer into his side and he crashed to the sand bleating like a sheep with its throat cut. "Captain" I announced, pinning his head in place by putting my boot on his remaining horn "I'm relieving you of command." Brock's face exploded as Chloe and I emptied our rifles into his face until he stopped twitching and his form desiccated and blew away as glittering dust.

I looked up the beach. Jaden was sitting in the sand with his dead sister's head in his lap.

Further along, the monsters danced together like awkward teens in an Annette Funicello beach movie. And I remembered the power was still ours, really.

Kutada read my intentions, and smiled with understanding, as if to say I finally got it.

I turned to Chloe and told her that our flesh keys could still be put to good use.

We could make the world a better place.

Laura, we can do this.

The sunlight hit its zenith as Chloe and I stood over Laura's body. Jaden stood off to the side, shuffling awkwardly as we wriggled out of our tights, crusty from the weirdest, most wrong night sequence of adventures ever. Jaden just wanted his sister alive again, so he was willing to trust our new and hard-won power.

Chloe understood more of what I wanted, finally, and we had undergone a role reversal. She spit on her prick, as did I, pressed straight onto mine and we started the ancient ritual that predates religion itself. Time was of the essence, because we wanted to resurrect Laura before her brain and body stopped working.

I stopped thinking about the exclusivity of Chloe. I had been blind to my need for loving my tribe from my disillusionment in New York. Finally love and *being* filled my heart, brain, and dick—Chloe recognized my breakthrough, found the same things in herself, and followed my lead. Our pricks got even harder as she attacked me with her lips and we squeezed even closer.

"We're finally doing this," I told my erstwhile mentor. "Are you ready?"

"Let's go," Chloe smiled, not minding that her makeup had sweated off. I didn't mind it, either.

An electricity took our bodies over as the floodgates opened and as he pressed and gyrated together in the warm Pacific breeze and hot white sand, Chloe and I looked into each other's eyes and knew we were about to perform a crazily unprecedented and beautiful miracle.

"Ready?" I asked her.

"Born ready. So is Laura."

Right before the floodgates opened up, we both turn to Laura's supine body, and in harmonious divination, we came onto her chest wound, and then we shook the dregs of our hot whey across her tits. The cum glistened there in the sun a moment, then joined its stringy viscous friends in stitching Laura's life force back together.

Chloe asked me if we were making a zombie.

"No," I said. "We're making a trinity."

My voice sounded really low, but perfectly confident.

That was a nice change.

Laura opened her eyes, hawked up a wad of sperm, spat and smiled. "What the *fuck* just happened?"

Roz was leading my parents over for a reunion, but

I couldn't even bring myself to care. I grabbed Laura by the hair and kissed her on the mouth. "You're back, don't you want to thank me and Chloe?"

Laura dutifully brought her face down to my dick and began devouring it like a drowning woman gasping for air. Her gasps intensified when Chloe came up behind her, split her ass and pushed her face forward till she gagged, gluing her mouth to mine.

Pausing to bite Chloe's lip awhile Laura slaved away at pleasing the two of us, I started forming the contours of a plan, refusing to be interrupted by my parents and sister awkwardly coughing and trying to get my attention while averting their eyes and dragging their feet in the sand. "Chloe, Laura, we have access to monsters and control over The Sway—how about we become monsters? Really go with it just level every city, smash The Rattites, just remake the world in our image… Don't you think… That would be great?" I inquired as I began spasming along with Chloe and Laura, cum dripping from Laura's mouth and ass mixing with the ichor, blood and shattered crab dogs in the sand. "Wouldn't it be great to destroy the whole fucking world?"

Torrents of white-hot cream filled the already salty island breeze, another noise came from the lagoon.

Janssen wormed onto the beach from the toxic waters. He was still wrapped in cling wrap head to toe. Even without his teeth, it was easy enough to understand him when he questioned us.

"What'd I miss?"

Larissa Glasser is a librarian, metalhead, and queerAF trans woman from Boston. She is a Member at Large of Broad Universe, which promotes, educates, and advocates for female-identified writers of genre fiction. She is on Twitter @larissaeglasser. This is her first novella.

F4
Larissa Glasser

A cruise ship on the back of a sleeping kaiju. A transgender bartender trying to come terms with who she is. A rift in dimensions known as The Sway. A cruel captain. A storm of turmoil, insanity and magic is coming together and taking the ship deep into the unknown. What will Carol the bartender learn in this maddening non-place that changes bodies and minds alike into bizarre terrors? What is the sleeping monster who holds up the ship trying to tell her? What do Carol's fractured sense of self and a community of internet trolls have to do with the sudden pull of The Sway?

Polymer
Caleb Wilson

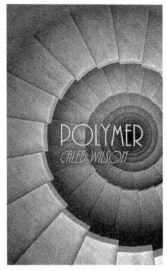

You've seen monster hunts before. You've watched as a guy with throwing axes and ninja stars ascends stairs to fight a big furry werewolf with tentacles or a floating head of indeterminate origin. You've seen hunters. But you've never seen Polymer. Polymer's got style, Polymer's got sex appeal, Polymer's got panache. And you, lucky reader, get to join us right behind the glass in Sickleburg Castle where the battle of the century is about to commence. Who is the man behind the music, the monsters, the guts, the gore and the glory? Get ready for an event like no other.

Winnie
Katy Michelle Quinn

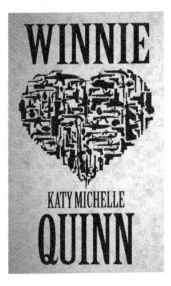

Winnie and Colt forever. Winnie is Colt's one and only, Colt is Winnie's true love. Winnie is Colt's rifle. There is nothing Winnie wants more than to please Colt and since a rifle is everything the young cowboy's ever wanted, she certainly does that. But one day Winnie finds that she is not a rifle but in fact a woman. Can Winnie keep the sparks between them ignited, even if she isn't the gun of his dreams. What happens if she can't?

Eviscerator
Farah Rose Smith

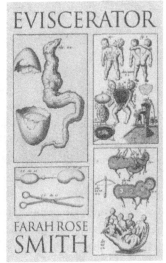

Vex Valis—doctor. Vex Valis—rocker. Vex Valis—iconoclast. You would think Vex Valis has it all but what Vex has is a secret that rots away at her from her very core. Vex is infected with Gut Ghouls and will do anything to be rid of them, even if it means consorting with subterranean worms or blending science and the occult in dangerous and unsavory ways. You may envy Vex's jet setting Dark Wave scientist lifestyle but you won't when you see the trials incurred when she catches the attention of a being that rends people and worlds alike, the scrutiny of…The Eviscerator

Fell Beauties
Leigham Shardlow

In the last outpost of ugliness in the world, beautiful people are falling from the sky. When Fat Janet is kicked out of the buffet where she has holed up for food and safety, she is forced to confront not only the reality of perfect falling bodies but the attentions of an overzealous plastic surgeon and his followers. She teams up with a mystery man in hopes of getting out of this alive but soon finds that confronting the problem head on is the only option. Can imperfection survive this beautiful disaster?

Crime of the Scene
Shawn Koch

A detective investigating a crime scene finds that nested inside this crime scene is another, and inside that another. Demons, physical deformity, body switching and endless trials await him as he begins to face his own transgressions. Reality grows distant as he soon comes to realize that he has stumbled not only upon the scene of many crimes but of all crimes. He might just have what it takes to get to the bottom of these but only if he gets to the bottom of himself.